THE GOVERNORS' ISLAND
Gwynn's Island, Virginia, During the Revolution

by

Peter Jennings Wrike

The Gwynn's Island Museum
Gwynn, Virginia

All illustrations done by author based on
sources listed in bibliography.
Text prepared by Elaine B. Dawson of Old
Dominion University in Norfolk, Virginia.
Text composed in Baskerville.

Library of Congress Cataloging-in-Publication Data
Wrike, Peter Jennings
The Governors' Island
Includes bibliographical references and index.
1. Virginia—History—Revolution

ISBN 1-883911-01-X (cloth)

Published by Brandylane Publishers in cooperation with
the Gwynn's Island Museum

Dedication

In memory of those who died during the Gwynn's Island campaign:

> The Count d'Arundel (usually called Captain Dohicky Arundel), Continental Army Artillery;

> Mr. Andrew Sprowl, one of colonial Virginia's leading citizens and founder of the Gosport shipyard;

> The scores of sailors, marines, militia and civilians both in "the floating town" and on the shore;

> And the hundreds of Dunmore's Royal Ethiopians, their families and dependents.

Contents

List of Illustrations

Figure

Preface

Mr. Wrike's account of the end of Royal Rule in Virginia takes us back to an older, simpler America. When I was a boy my grandfather would point proudly at a reproduction of a painting titled "The Spirit of '76." I, along with the rest of my generation viewed such an unself-critical display with chagrin—at best. Yet here, the reader encounters through Mr. Wrike's work the very disembodied essence the artist strove to convey in that painting.

We have a detailed retelling of Lord Dunmore's decline in power and authority. It is, and was, a long way from the governor's palace in Williamsburg to living on a ship in Norfolk harbor. This is followed by another demotion—to Gwynn's Island anchorage—and finally to being driven off entirely by the riff-raff, the hoi-polloi, Dunmore so despised.

This is a marvelous story, not just an historical account. We have all the elements of literature: a beginning, a middle, and an end; a conflict—who shall rule: the royal governor or the people? a climax: the ignominious departure of Dunmore's fleet from Gwynn's Island; a "villain"—the churlish Lord Dunmore lacks only a black high silk hat and cape; a collective hero: "the people," whom Dunmore so despised; and finally a theme: the underdog who turns and fights and wins! Throughout we have action, danger, fear, devotion, loyalty, double-dealing, and betrayal. It is a veritable swash-buckler, and, even better, it is all true. It is us! It is all our myths come to life!

Once upon a time a part would have been written to include Errol Flynn. I wonder who might be available today . . .

R. A. Doré
Gallows Bay
St. Croix, U.S.V.I.

Introduction

In the smallest rural county on the Chesapeake Bay in Virginia lies the tiny hamlet of Cricket Hill. Like many small villages and towns there is a long story associated with the name Cricket Hill. The name has nothing to do with crickets but much to do with American independence. Cricket Hill overlooks Gwynn's Island, the last bastion of Virginia's Royal Governor, John Murray, Lord Dunmore. Dunmore fortified the island from an armada of over one hundred Royal Navy and British loyalist vessels. For two months Dunmore led an aggressive campaign against Virginia and Maryland. During his campaign Dunmore purportedly compared the patriots' to "crickets on a hill" since the noise from their camp disturbed the Governor's sleep. The name Cricket Hill long survived the Governor.

There are a variety of reliable accounts of this time and the activities of many people involved. Only a handful of historians have carefully examined and analyzed the available records of Gwynn's Island in 1776. Professor John Selby, of the College of William and Mary, Dr. William Bell Morgan, Dr. Harold Moorman, Mr. Brent Tartar, and Dr. Peter Caley are scholars of the events and individuals of this period. Yet no single comprehensive account has addressed the efforts of Dunmore to establish a base of operations in Virginia to retake his colony. This book provides an account of Virginia loyalist and patriot activity connected with Dunmore's operations from Gwynn's Island.

While accounts of Dunmore's activities exist, each has a

different perspective and correlation of the events is often difficult.
It is that diversity of accounts that makes the campaign around
Gwynn's Island interesting. Most of the accounts reveal the
thoughts and emotions of individuals who, as the proverbial blind
men, describe their particular portion of the huge, elephant-like
Gwynn's Island campaign. Much of the work of this book has been
to make allowances for the exaggerations, resolve the inaccuracies,
and align the various accounts. In general *The Governors' Island*
follows a chronological format. This provides a convenient method
of interrelating the accounts. It also reveals the day-to-day nature
of the campaign.

Many accounts of Virginia during the early phases of the
American Revolution minimize the role of Dunmore and his
accomplishments. A few fail to mention Dunmore's efforts in 1775
and 1776 altogether, several mention his activities in Norfolk and
end there, and those that address the Gwynn's Island campaign
view it as a "last stand." That was not the prevailing view in 1776.
Today we look at those events with the advantage of hindsight, yet
Dunmore's efforts to crush the rebellion in his colony, as well as
the British to do the same in North America, might have
succeeded.

Dunmore's efforts to recapture Virginia were vigorous but
unsupported. Eventually his resources evaporated but not through
battle, capture or desertion. Dunmore chose Gwynn's Island to
erect his standard, build a powerful base of operations, and gather
an army for the reconquest of Virginia. This more detailed
presentation reveals the effects of individual decisions as well as
circumstances on the conduct of that campaign. The ending
doesn't change but readers should find this work presents more
clearly those events in Virginia in May, June, July, and August
1776.

The Floating Town

George Washington called him the most dangerous man in America. John Adams thought he needed to be stopped and quickly. Thomas Jefferson both vilified and immortalized him in the Declaration of Independence when he wrote:

> He had abdicated government here, by declaring us out of his protection, and waging war against us. He has plundered our seas, ravaged our coasts, burnt our towns and destroyed the lives of our people. He has constrained our fellow citizens, taken captive on the high seas, to bear arms against their country, to become the executioners of their friends, and brethren, or to fall themselves by their hands. He has excited domestic insurrections amongst us, and has endeavored to bring on the inhabitants of our frontiers, the merciless indian savages.[1]

Washington, Adams and Jefferson referred to John Murray, Lord Dunmore, last Royal Governor of Virginia.

Dunmore did all that Jefferson wrote, and more. Dunmore strongly supported the British colonists loyal to the crown while he aggressively maintained an offensive against those he considered rebels. From April 1775 through July 1776, Dunmore raised a considerable military and naval force which disrupted trade in the entire Chesapeake Bay region; he fought, imprisoned and killed colonial militia; he seized and destroyed vast quantities of military and civilian property; he emancipated Virginia's slaves and then recruited and armed them; and he gathered about him thousands of American loyalists. At the same time, Dunmore actively sought military support from the British Government to more vigorously prosecute the war.

The British Government supported the idea that the royal governors should restore order in their rebellious colonies. The British and the colonists had different opinions on the course of the rebellion. In the winter of 1775, Britain searched for soldiers, preferably foreign, to reinforce the colonial governors. Britain did not want to use British troops against British colonists in a war. The prospect of war against the colonies was unpopular in Britain and some British colonies appeared reluctant to actively and fully participate in the rebellion. In the summer of 1775, the colonists sent the Olive Branch petition to King George III, which sought mediation of the rebellion. The King rejected the petition. In the colonies, loyalists still openly supported the royal governors and even greater numbers of loyalists secretly professed allegiance to the King. Many erstwhile loyalists stated their ability to openly support the King was dependent solely on the restoration of royal authority. To the King's ministers and the royal governors, the solution to the American rebellion appeared simple. The ministers planned to equip and arm the loyalists, provide a small mercenary army for support, provide sufficient naval protection and transport, and encourage the royal governors to retake their colonies. The southern colonies offered the best site for this strategy and limited British resources. The governors of Virginia, North Carolina, South Carolina and Georgia all had strong loyalist support, some militia forces, command of the sea, and appeared eager to regain control of their colonies. Of all the colonial governors, Dunmore of Virginia waged the most aggressive campaign to retake his colony.[2]

Dunmore governed the largest and wealthiest British colony in North America. Virginia geographically separated the southern colonies from the Northern. Virginia controlled the entrance to the Chesapeake Bay. The Bay provided deep water access to the interior of Virginia, Maryland, Delaware, and Pennsylvania. At the mouth of the Bay the port of Hampton Roads was the largest and finest harbor south of New York. The cities of Portsmouth,

Hampton and Norfolk surrounded Hampton Roads. Norfolk ranked among the largest British cities in North America. In Portsmouth, loyalist Andrew Sprowl administered the largest shipyard in the colonies. Most of the lucrative colonial tobacco trade sailed from the Chesapeake to England and Scotland. The Chesapeake region's strong trade with the West Indies brought needed staples as well as luxuries to the region. A Virginia loyal to the King would greatly facilitate an end to the rebellion.

Governor Dunmore developed a sound strategy to retake Virginia. He gathered his limited military forces and loyalist supporters on vessels based in Hampton Roads. From there, loyalist privateers cruised the Bay and the Atlantic coast from Georgia to Delaware. These privateers seized colonial vessels on the slightest pretext, brought supplies back to Dunmore, and greatly diminished water-borne trade in the region. Backed by powerful units of the Royal Navy, Dunmore's naval forces outmanned and outgunned the meager Virginia State Navy as well as the infant Continental Navy. Dunmore controlled the waters over which troops, loyalists, and supplies reached his "floating town." Over those same waters Dunmore dispatched raiding parties and military forces to disrupt or destroy potential opponents. Dunmore first planned to regain control of Virginia. Later, he broadened his strategy to support other southern governors, including Eden of Maryland, in their reconquest efforts. To achieve his strategy, Dunmore recruited loyalists and requested more regular troops.[3]

Alarmed at Dunmore's activity, the patriot forces gathered strength around Hampton Roads and eventually curbed his efforts to militarily control the region. Intimidated and isolated by the patriots, Dunmore evacuated all his forces in late May of 1776. Under Royal Navy leadership, a fleet of over one hundred vessels left Hampton Roads and sailed up the Chesapeake Bay. The fleet carried Royal Navy sailors, Royal Marines, British Army troops, loyalist regiments, patriot prisoners, civilian loyalists, indentured servants, and slaves. Many of the fleet's inhabitants were accompanied by their families. After a short, unopposed passage, the fleet anchored in the mouth of the Piankatank River, just off Gwynn's Island. Troops landed on the three square mile island, constructed fortifications, set up a large military camp, established a hospital, built ovens for bread and food production, and erected tents to house the fleet's growing population of almost two thousand persons. Later, the Royal Governor of Maryland joined Dunmore on the island. For a short time, tiny Gwynn's Island became the seat of British royal authority for Virginia and Maryland. From Gwynn's Island, Dunmore attempted to subdue the rebels and lead the campaign to restore royal authority in Virginia, Maryland and eventually British North America.

Dunmore arrived in Virginia in 1771 from the governorship of New York. He succeeded the popular Governor Lord Botetourt. Dunmore had served less than a year in New York, and was very upset at his reassignment to Virginia. Despite his ire, Dunmore knew that Virginia provided the best governor's post in British North America. As in New York, Dunmore used his position in Virginia to advance his own interests, particularly claims to western lands. Dunmore was not the first nor was he the only speculator. He does seem to be more avaricious than most. At the same time he was speculating in western land claims, he was enforcing British edicts which forbad western settlement by the colonists.[4]

In 1774, Dunmore led an expedition (known as Dunmore's War) against the Indians in western Virginia. White settlement in that region pressured the Indians who felt protected by treaty. Despite Dunmore's enforcement, new settlers arrived. The French had traditionally encouraged the Indians to attack British settlements. That threat ended in 1763 but Indian enmity toward whites in general and British in particular, persisted. The expedition's success owed more to the colonists' support than Dunmore's leadership. Dunmore conducted the campaign personally, but shared the success with the veteran Virginia Commander, Colonel Andrew Lewis. In the final action, Andrew Lewis's brother Charles died in battle. Many western Virginians felt Dunmore did not participate in the war as aggressively as had others. Many felt that Dunmore's expedition not only protected the settlers but also the Governor's personal interests. Lewis, like other Virginians, suspected Dunmore's motives. Lewis was also deeply troubled by the loss of his brother.[5]

The concerns of the western Virginians were shared by many in Tidewater. Some wealthy Tidewater Virginians, such as George

Washington and others of more moderate means, also speculated in western lands. Yet many Tidewater Virginians thought Dunmore's apparent preoccupation with the western part of the colony hurt their interests. Merchants and business interests fared badly under the colonial trade embargoes. Dunmore's absence on western matters allowed the local merchant associations and Committee of Safety to restrain trade. The Tidewater interests wanted the Governor to shift his focus to their problems.

Both western and Tidewater interests harbored grievances against Dunmore. When he returned to Williamsburg in late 1774, American nationalist feeling pressured British colonial rule. In a time of political, social and economic change, the governor and other incumbents became convenient targets for the opposition. Many persons who otherwise supported the Crown, were intimidated by the "mob."

Though open rebellion had not occurred in Virginia in early 1775, tensions ran high. Shortly after his return from the Indian campaign, Dunmore precipitated a conflict with his citizenry by removing gunpowder from the magazine in Williamsburg. The incident occurred less than two days after the skirmishes at Lexington and Concord. Though they had not yet learned of the Massachusetts incidents, local citizens reacted strongly to Dunmore's seizure of the powder, and he did nothing to ease tensions. For the next six weeks, Dunmore isolated himself in the Governor's Palace in Williamsburg.[6]

Unable to control the events in New England and fearing the same in Virginia, Dunmore fled with his family to HMS *Fowey* in Yorktown on June 8, 1775. Later the Virginia assembly met with him on board the *Fowey*, but the Governor was intransigent. He prorogued the Assembly and in essence, declared martial law in Virginia.[7]

At Williamsburg, the situation further deteriorated. Dunmore's absence and continued hard line for control of Virginia worried his supporters, polarized moderates and confirmed the worst suspicions of the Whigs who supported independence. The assembly declared that Dunmore had abandoned office. Dunmore sent his family back to England and, in early July 1775, he moved the *Fowey* and several small vessels with loyalist sympathizers to Hampton Roads. This became the nucleus of Governor Dunmore's support in Virginia. Their presence made his governorship viable.

Dunmore's presence in Hampton Roads caused further problems for the area's merchants. While Dunmore had remained in Williamsburg or Yorktown, business in Hampton Roads continued with a series of arrangements. The growing conflict in New England severely disrupted trade there and other colonial ports, such as Norfolk, benefitted from the problems in Boston. Overseas consumption continued unabated and prices for Virginia goods rose. The colony's merchants generally enforced the embargoes passed by the assembly. However, some merchants ignored or only casually acknowledged the embargoes. While the local citizens and Committees of Safety increasingly called merchants to account for their activities, merchants dominated the business, society and politics of Norfolk and Hampton Roads. Prosecutions were few and the authority of the Committees more coercive than punitive. Dunmore's arrival in July 1775 made it difficult to continue these "handshake arrangements." Dunmore took a hard line against the "rebels" and he vigorously prosecuted those merchants who traded with them.

Dunmore's presence in Hampton Roads required courtesies and civilities from his supporters. However, those who entertained the Governor were seen by the populace as loyalists and a "danger to liberty." Those who openly collaborated with the Governor were often ostracized. Some endured the pressure; some went to the Eastern Shore of Virginia and Maryland; several left for England and Scotland; and many others joined Dunmore in the harbor of Hampton Roads.[8]

Many local merchants owned vessels. They placed their families and treasured items on board their vessels and anchored in the harbor. At first, this was not a radical step. The heat of summer, smallpox, yellow fever and other calamities had in the past driven Hampton Roads residents to the water for relief, isolation, or self-imposed quarantine. They would remain until the problem subsided and then return to their homes. While aboard their vessels, goods arrived from shore, servants watched their possessions and business continued to be conducted. In the summer of 1775, those who joined Dunmore's "floating town" were blissfully unaware of the duration of their quarantine.

As the summer of 1775 progressed, Virginians realized that

the rebellion to the North threatened to engulf all the colonies. In the South the royal governments of North Carolina, South Carolina, and later Georgia also administered their colonies from Royal Navy vessels offshore. Dunmore's presence in the harbor not only restricted trade but hurt the long-standing traffic in non-dutied items—smuggling. As legal and extra-legal trade declined, the economic situation grew worse. The empty homes of loyalists also provided opportunities to vent frustrations through burning and vandalism.[9]

Soon after Dunmore arrived in Hampton Roads, Virginia militia gathered onshore to prevent raids by the loyalists. Their presence antagonized the loyalists and pressured moderates. As more loyalists joined Dunmore, the fleet's need for shore replenishment grew. As more loyalists and sympathizers left Virginia, fewer were available to help those in the fleet. The militia gradually tightened the watch on the harbor and fewer supplies reached the "floating town." The necessity for supplies, particularly water, increased the frequency and severity of raids by forces under Dunmore's command. It was not yet warfare but an uneasy tension between the fleet and the shore with the loyalties of those on shore divided. Occasional violence punctuated the tension.[10]

As more loyalists joined Dunmore the fleet grew, while the Virginia militia also increased its numbers. Each confrontation and every skirmish escalated the tension. In October 1775, regular British troops from the 14th Regiment at St. Augustine reinforced Dunmore. Dunmore then led a large expedition ashore, similar to Gage's disastrous expedition to Lexington and Concord. The results were better. The British met and routed the patriot militia at Kemp's Landing. On the spot some local citizens and a number of the defeated militia swore allegiance to the King. When Dunmore arrived back in Norfolk, another 200 citizens swore allegiance to the King. Shortly before the Battle at Kemp's Landing, Dunmore boldly seized the patriot press in Norfolk which published the *Virginia Gazette*. Soon the weekly newspaper reflected Dunmore's editorial policies and a decidedly loyalist slant to current events in Virginia.[11]

On November 14th, Dunmore effectively emancipated many of Virginia's slaves. He needed more troops and enlisted the freed slaves in his newly created Dunmore's Royal Ethiopian Regiment.

Figure 1 Chesapeake Bay Region

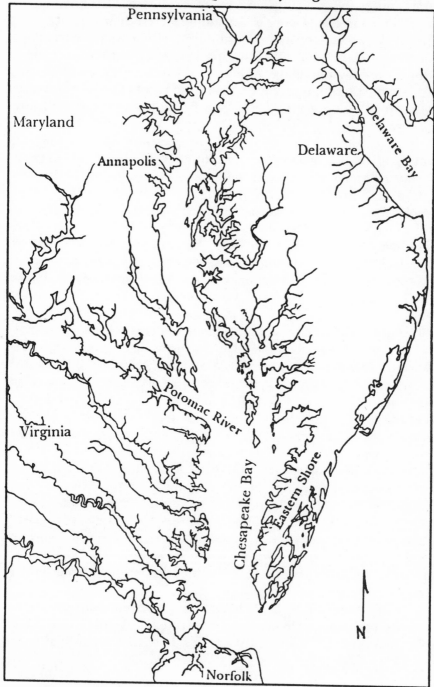

Figure 2 Hampton Roads

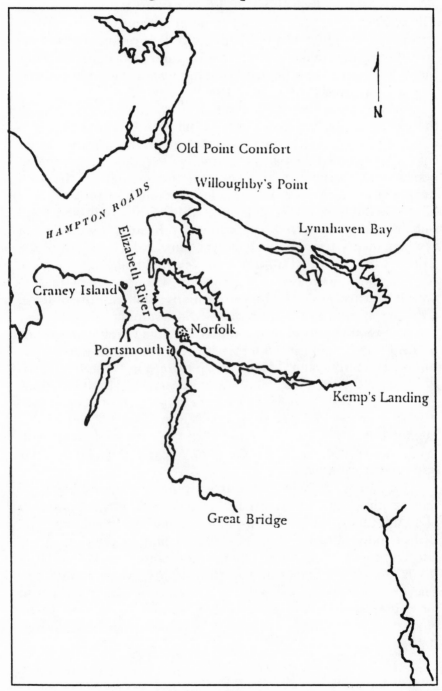

That regiment performed many functions and also fought alongside regular British troops. White officers led the regiment. The emancipation of slaves and creation of the Royal Ethiopians angered and frightened Virginians. Outside Virginia, southerners and northerners alike considered Dunmore's actions extreme. More Virginians were polarized by the emancipation and many now were arrayed against Dunmore.[12]

In early December 1775, Dunmore's troops marched to attack the patriot militia at Great Bridge. The British hoped to gain a decisive victory before cannon and regular troops from other colonies reinforced the patriots. Dunmore executed the campaign poorly, and the patriots inflicted severe casualties on the 14th Regiment in particular. Dunmore lost the initiative on land, and he was forced to go on the defensive. Most of the loyalists who still remained ashore moved to Dunmore's floating town. Patriot reinforcements arrived and lined the harbor. Harassment of the British, which included sniping from deserted buildings along the Norfolk shore, increased. In retaliation, Dunmore sent raiding parties selectively to several shore locations to kill, capture or drive away the snipers. Each raid redoubled the sniping.[13]

The regular patriot troops under Virginia Colonel Woodford disliked the situation in Hampton Roads. The floating town was still supplied from shore. Many of the citizens in Hampton Roads still had strong economic, family, and personal ties to the loyalists. Woodford's troops were from the western part of the state. These frontiersmen saw Norfolk as materialistic in character and loyalist in sympathy. They reasoned if the town was destroyed, the British would be forced to leave. On New Year's Day 1776, their opportunity came.

On January 1, 1776 British troops, under covering fire from the warships, landed troops in Norfolk and burned deserted buildings along the wharf suspected of harboring snipers. The British moved swiftly and encountered little opposition. They burned nineteen buildings. The burning caused confusion. High winds fanned the flames and spread the fire to other buildings. The disenchanted militia seized the opportunity and set fire to more buildings. Militia forces either burned or allowed to be burned 863 buildings. Many of Norfolk's public buildings, businesses and private homes disappeared in the three day blaze. The fifth largest city in British North America no longer existed.[14]

While patriot commanders fully understood their troops' role in the town's destruction, the British were blamed, and few patriots clarified the facts. Many of the homeless townspeople left for the surrounding counties to live with family or friends. Norfolk's destruction virtually eliminated the sniping. However, it made supply of the fleet from shore more difficult. The burned and deserted waterfront clearly revealed any activity. American forces more easily observed small craft which left the shore or moved to and from the fleet.

News of Norfolk's destruction worried colonists in Boston, New York, Philadelphia and Charleston. Two months earlier the British had burned Falmouth (now Portland), Maine. Now the British appeared to have burned Norfolk, even though it housed many loyalists. Other towns could perish the same way. The struggle with Great Britain became more grim after Norfolk was burned. The destruction of a city gave a new and terrifying dimension to the colonists' understanding of warfare.

The British and Americans skirmished several times in late January and early February 1776. British forces landed and burned a few additional buildings used by snipers to annoy the fleet. On February 6, North Carolina Militia Colonel Howe withdrew all but 300 troops and moved west to Suffolk. As Howe withdrew, he burned 416 buildings that remained in Norfolk. In a little over five weeks Norfolk lost 1,298 buildings. This left virtually all the town's population of 6,000 homeless.[15]

Powerful reinforcements reached Dunmore only three days after Howe completed the final burning of Norfolk. The 44-gun frigate HMS *Roebuck* and several escorts arrived in Hampton Roads. Veteran Royal Navy Captain Andrew S. Hamond commanded the new warship, its 100 marines and 260-man crew. No Continental or state navy warship came close in size, firepower, and discipline. The *Roebuck*'s arrival altered Congressional plans for an attack on Dunmore by the fledgling Continental Navy. The Continental fleet, under Esek Hopkins, originally received orders to attack Dunmore in December 1775. Delays prevented Hopkins' sailing until February. By then Hamond had reinforced Dunmore. After he learned of the *Roebuck*'s arrival, Hopkins decided not to attack Dunmore, and he led the Continental fleet to the Bahamas on a raid.[16]

Captain Hamond and Governor Dunmore had known each other previously. In 1772, Hamond commanded the 32-gun frigate, HMS *Arethusa*. While the *Arethusa* underwent lengthy repairs at Andrew Sprowl's shipyard in Gosport (now Portsmouth), Virginia, Captain Hamond and Governor Dunmore developed a friendship. Dunmore first encouraged and then approved a claim for Hamond to receive almost 20,000 acres of Virginia's Western lands. Eventually, the British government disallowed Hamond's Virginia claim.[17]

Howe's withdrawal and Hamond's arrival greatly encouraged Dunmore. Under Royal Navy protection Dunmore landed and occupied Tucker's Point in Portsmouth. He put a windmill for making flour back into service. Dunmore built ovens for making bread and dug wells. He also built barracks on shore to relieve overcrowding in the fleet. Those conditions promoted disease, and, at this time, smallpox cases were discovered. One of the barracks became a hospital. Dunmore also fortified the Point and dug a defensive line which separated the Point from the mainland. The British now had a land base and control of the sea. Dunmore appeared to be firmly in command at Hampton Roads. A week after Hamond's arrival, a British task force with three troopships and support vessels entered Hampton Roads. General Sir Henry Clinton, commander of British forces in North America, paused in Virginia to make repairs to his vessels.[18]

Dunmore was initially elated and thought Clinton brought him long sought reinforcements. Dunmore's elation quickly turned to surprise and then anger. Clinton was en route to join forces with Charles, Lord Cornwallis, to attack North Carolina. Governor Tryon of New York, formerly governor of North Carolina, and Governor Martin of North Carolina had assured Clinton of tremendous loyalist support in North Carolina. Clinton decided to support Martin. Dunmore immediately wrote a caustic letter to London and spoke derisively of the plan. He called North Carolina "a most insignificant province" as compared to Virginia, which was "the first Colony of the Continent, both for Riches and Power."[19]

During Clinton's stay, he attended a meeting on the *Roebuck* between Dunmore and Virginia's Receiver General, Richard

Corbin. Corbin wanted Dunmore to convene the General Assembly and sought mediation of Virginia's problems through Clinton. Corbin suggested Dunmore, as governor, lead the assembly himself or delegate that authority to Thomas Nelson. Both Clinton and Dunmore were unresponsive to Corbin's suggestion.

While Corbin met with Clinton in Hampton Roads, the Committee of Safety and the Virginia Convention in Williamsburg took action to improve the colony's military preparedness. The Convention created six new regiments which were then taken into the Continental line. Veteran Colonel Andrew Lewis became a Continental Brigadier General. The popular but thin-skinned militia colonel Patrick Henry resigned in protest to Lewis's promotion. Soon after his visit with Dunmore, Clinton sailed south to rendezvous with troops and naval support in Wilmington. After arrival there events changed Clinton's final destination to Charleston, South Carolina.[20]

In Philadelphia Congress appointed Major General Charles Lee to command the Southern Department of the Continental Army. In late March of 1776, Lee arrived in Williamsburg. There he developed a strategy to defend the South against Clinton's expedition. Lee wanted to improve Virginia's military forces and take more vigorous action against Dunmore. Clinton's final destination was still unclear, and Dunmore appeared strong. Shortly after Lee's arrival, captured dispatches between London and Governor Eden of Maryland revealed Eden's willingness to forcefully crush the rebellion. Dunmore was Eden's nearest support. Dunmore's strength and Eden's loyalist sympathies worried Lee. Lee ordered a complete evacuation of the entire harbor of Hampton Roads for three miles inland. This would deprive the loyalists of support and supplies. Lee also recommended Portsmouth be burned and known loyalists arrested.[21]

Through April of 1776, the Virginia Convention acted slowly on Lee's recommendations. Lee did not hesitate. He used his Continental authority and resources to improve Virginia's defenses. Some of his actions, such as his use of the Governor's Palace for a personal residence and the College of William and Mary as a hospital offended Virginians. He remained unaffected. In early May, news reached Lee of Clinton's movements further

south and Lee headed to Charleston to direct the Continental
forces. His efforts to pressure Dunmore had animated the local
militia. Patriot pressure on Dunmore continued.[22]

The patriots' efforts worried Dunmore. Hamond and the
Roebuck had sailed in April to the Delaware River to attack
American forces around Philadelphia. Dunmore sent a letter to
Hamond and asked him to return to Virginia. The Governor
wrote of his fears and urgent need for naval protection.
Meanwhile, their mission on the Delaware completed, Hamond
and the *Roebuck* started south to join Clinton's expedition.

2

The Island

Gwynn's Island entered history as part of the legend of the Indian maiden Pocahontas, daughter of Chief Powhatan, the powerful head of Tidewater's Indian tribes. The legend, still repeated in the twentieth century, credited the English colonist, Hugh Gwynn, with the rescue of Pocahontas from drowning in the Piankatank River. In gratitude, Pocahontas gave Gwynn a nearby island. The island became known as Gwynn's Island.

In the early 1600s, the Powhatan Indian Confederation ruled the region around Gwynn's Island. Powhatan reserved the island, nearby land and surrounding waters as a hunting preserve. The village of the nearest Confederation tribe, the Piankatanks, lay several miles upriver from the island. Pocahontas married the English colonist John Rolfe and died while on a visit to England in 1617. One year later Powhatan died and his kinsman, Opecancanough, became chief of the powerful Tidewater Indian Confederation.[1]

Gwynn's Island remained under Indian control. Opecancanough led a well-organized surprise attack on the Virginia colonists in 1622. The attack almost succeeded, and a third of Virginia's colonists died. As a consequence both of that attack and administrative changes in the colony, the English government restricted further development of the region. Settlement in the Gwynn's Island area was strongly discouraged and technically illegal.

In 1635, Virginia colonist Hugh Gwynn made a claim to King

Charles I of England for property on Gwynn's Island as well as the
adjacent mainland. Charles I faced many serious domestic and
foreign difficulties which required his full attention. Nonetheless,
he finally granted Gwynn's claim in 1640. Gwynn, along with
Abraham English, John Lilly, Peter Rigby and John Congdon
shared property which bordered the protected waters between the
island and the mainland known as Milford Haven. Gwynn's initial
grant included almost one quarter of the island.[2]

Opecancanough led another attack on the Virginia colonists
in 1644. This attack killed more settlers than in 1622, but the
colony's population was now much larger. The colonists'
successfully counterattacked; Opecancanough was captured, and
severe reprisals made by the settlers. As Opecancanough awaited
trial, an angry settler killed the aged chief. After 1644, the Indians'
right to hold land in the region eroded, and by 1652 it had
disappeared.

Colonel Hugh Gwynn claimed an additional 500 acres in
1652, of which 300 acres was on the "west side of a tract called
Gwins Island . . . being the surplusage of said island, bounded
southwest upon the Narrowes, west opposite to the mouth of the
Piankatank River, south upon Deep Creek which lyeth toward
south side of said island." The following year Gwynn's 1700 acres
went from "Sandy Poynt that butts upon Chesapeake Bay,
extending up Milford Haven Bay unto the Narrows . . ." This
acreage included creeks, marsh, "indian fields" and woods. Nearby
one Richard Burton patented land west of the island.[3]

Colonel Hugh Gwynn represented his neighbors as a burgess
in Virginia's assembly in 1639, 1646 and 1652. He served as justice
of the peace, and his rank of colonel made him one of the colony's
senior militia officers. He prospered in business, and he took a
strong role in establishing and maintaining the Anglican Church
in the parish. Gwynn built a home and lived on Gwynn's Island by
1635. His home on Milford Haven used the materials at hand. The
island's forests provided framing material for a story and a half
house. Rough clapboard siding covered the frame. Local clay
became bricks with a minimum of skill. Indentured servants did
much of the labor. Outbuildings included a kitchen, dairy, barn,
servants quarters and "necessary buildings." In addition, there

were boat sheds. The Gwynns traveled by water whether to church, court, Assembly, trade, visits or any other reason to leave the island. Self-sufficiency characterized Virginia colonists and island life increased that ability.[4]

The island was largely wooded, but as the land was cleared, its soil produced good crops. The island also created a natural pen for cattle, sheep and other livestock. Milford Haven provided a large, deep, protected anchorage for colonial vessels. It was a day's sail to Hampton Roads and about the same to the Maryland Colony. The island was easily recognized by passing vessels and lay opposite the narrowest point on the lower Chesapeake Bay. Tidal marshes, particularly on the island's east end, converted readily into "pans" which produced salt—the traditional preservative of meat and fish.

It took little imagination to turn these natural advantages to profit. Colonel Hugh Gwynn supplied passing vessels with a safe anchorage, water, preserved food and, eventually, vessel repairs. Gwynn rose to prominence in the Virginia colony through his industry. His royalist sympathies assured him of success in the conservative colony. The English Civil War (1642 to 1649) coincided with the peak of Gwynn's success. Many immigrants left England and came to Virginia. Maritime commerce increased as the colony's population and trade grew. Growth in the nearby Maryland colony further stimulated Virginia's trade. No commercial regulation existed in Hugh Gwynn's time. Vessels from abroad unloaded goods on the island, and then rested, resupplied and refitted for a return voyage. From the island, small sailing vessels as well as large native canoes carried the goods up the Piankatank and throughout the region.[5]

Colonel Hugh Gwynn was and always had been a King's man, but the execution of Charles I in 1649 brought Parliament to power. Even Virginia's Royal Governor Berkeley acknowledged the reign of Parliament, and the King's supporters in Virginia expected no favors from Parliament. When Gwynn died in 1654, his widow sold the mainland property and consolidated their island holdings. Abraham Moon's family acquired some of this property. Gwynn's death occurred as trade between England and her colonies declined. The years following her husband's death proved difficult for the widow and her family. England, Virginia and the Gwynns rejoiced when Charles II was crowned King in 1660.

With Charles II and the restoration of the monarchy came new opportunities, increased business, and regulation. At first, the impact of regulation scarcely mattered. The Navigation Acts regulated the colony's commerce, but they required enforcement—specifically, official ports and a customs establishment. Officials were easy to appoint, but where to put them in rural Tidewater remained a problem. Few towns of any consequence existed. The first effective steps to resolving the problem occurred in the 1680s. The colony's Assembly located six ports in Virginia for the transaction of maritime business. Gwynn's Island lay midway between the official ports of Urbanna and Yorktown. The island's strategic location afforded opportunities to transact maritime business without going to the official ports. References to "warehouses" on Gwynn's Island attest to the volume of trade handled there. Sometimes cargoes were partially unloaded on or near the island to smaller vessels. Often high-duty items were exchanged for goods with less duty. This avoidance of duties was prevalent in Virginia and other British colonies. To many colonists this practice was business as usual. The British called it smuggling.[6]

Since Hugh's death the Gwynn family had acquired more island property. By 1700, three Gwynn households held half of the island's 2,200 acres. The island lay at the northern end of Gloucester County in Kingston Parish. Kingston Parish was one of four parishes in Gloucester County, and it was almost completely surrounded by water. The numerous rivers, creeks and coves provided over two hundred miles of waterfront, including some marsh but much with firm, accessible shoreline. Gloucester County was a large and prosperous county in 1700. It had been strongly considered as Virginia's next capital after Jamestown burned in 1698. It lost that honor to Middle Plantation, later renamed Williamsburg, but Gloucester remained a force in Virginia politics.[7]

Restoration of the British monarchy, successful wars against the Dutch, and a growing maritime strength improved England's overseas commerce. Virginia's trade and business on Gwynn's Island grew proportionately. The increased prosperity of the

Gwynns and their eligible daughters attracted two other families to the island, the Keebles and Reades. These families acquired the other half of the island. The Keebles acquired island property as early as 1655 and lived adjacent to Cherry Point on Keeble Pond near the island's north shore. The Reades lived on the northeast side of the island, though they later occupied a Gwynn residence on the Haven. The Gwynns remained along Milford Haven. In 1704 approximately fifty people lived on the island. These included five families, their servants, and livestock including over 200 cattle, 100 sheep, a number of assorted pigs, chickens and other animals. The island residents enjoyed a high standard of living. Their location and business ensured an ample and varied diet. Finfish and shellfish abounded in the island's waters. Six-foot long sturgeon and dozens of other fish varieties swam in the island's waters. Oysters, clams and crabs could be harvested from shore.[8]

The island residents included many African-Americans as well as several white indentured servants. Much of the year the African-Americans harvested shellfish and finfish from local waters. All the island's inhabitants shared this harvest. The African-Americans had earned the Indians' trust and learned fishing skills from them. As Indians disappeared from the region, African-Americans continued to use the Indian's log canoe and modified the design for a variety of other needs. As many as a dozen log canoes served the island's transportation and fishing needs by the 1720s.

Late in the winter of 1729, six indentured servants fled from a nearby mainland plantation and hid for a few nights on the island. On the evening of March 4, the small trading sloop *John and Mary* anchored a short distance to the west of Gwynn's Island. Captain John Grymes and his mate and servant Alexander Abbott slept below decks on their cargo of hides. The next day they planned to complete their voyage to Norfolk, discharge the hides, and return to King George County on the upper Potomac. From the island, the runaways saw the *John and Mary* as an opportunity for a new life—as pirates. Under cover of darkness they stole one of the island log canoes, paddled to the sloop, and overpowered the captain and mate as they slept.[9]

In the morning, the amateur pirates surveyed their prize, cargo and captives. The pirates decided to use the small *John and*

Figure 3 Gwynn's Island

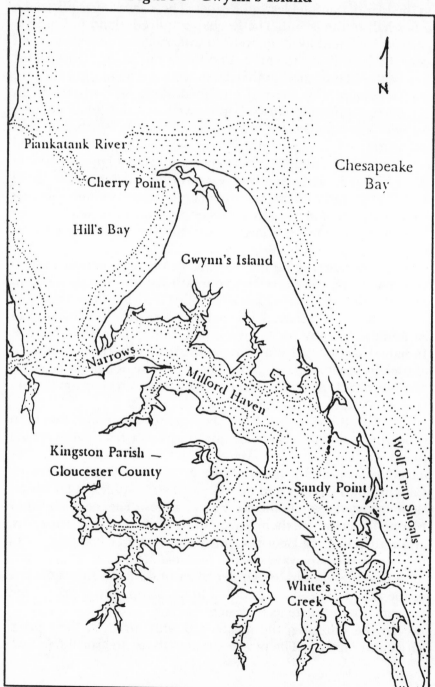

N

Piankatank River

Cherry Point

Hill's Bay

Gwynn's Island

Chesapeake Bay

Narrows

Milford Haven

Kingston Parish — Gloucester County

Sandy Point

Wolf Trap Shoals

White's Creek

Mary to capture a larger vessel on the Chesapeake. Then they planned to leave the Bay and begin a new career, like the infamous and recently executed Blackbeard. They hoisted the sloop's anchor and sailed around Gwynn's Island into the Chesapeake. The amateur pirates soon ran aground. With no knowledge of local waters or navigation, they forced the sloop's captain to help them sail. The amateur pirates decided to avoid the main shipping channel and search for small local vessels near the more remote shores. The *John and Mary* first cruised off Virginia's Eastern Shore with no success. Then the sloop cruised around Mobjack Bay—again with no success. During this time, the pirates vainly tried to convince the captain and mate to join their adventure—also with no success.

After two weeks, the frustrated pirates released their captives near Yorktown. They stripped them of their clothes and all possessions, then gave the captain three hides and the mate one hide to cover their nakedness.

Captain Grymes and mate Abbott quickly made their way ashore through the Guinea marshes of Gloucester County. Despite their nakedness, they found and convinced Mann Page of Rosewell of their story. Page, a powerful Colonial official, sent one of his small vessels to Yorktown and alerted the authorities. The amateur pirates were hunted down and captured. In August 1729, the court in Williamsburg heard their case. Edmund Williams, George Caves, George Cole (alias Sanders), Edward Edwards, Jeremiah Smith and Mary Critchett pled guilty to piracy.

The *John and Mary* incident was a consequence of Virginia's developing economy. Since the general European peace in 1714 colonial trade with the West Indies had grown. Declining prices for tobacco accelerated trade development in the West Indies. Corn, grain and naval products were staples of this trade and Norfolk became the trade's primary port for export and import. The West Indies trade increased in the 1730s and accelerated with the European wars after 1739. Vessels such as sloops, schooners, brigs and snows conveniently served both the Bay and the Indies trade. Opportunities expanded for able-bodied individuals to serve in the maritime trades. The enterprising Gwynns, Keebles and Reades built, owned, crewed and commanded these types of vessels in the West Indies trade.[10]

In the 1740s, Hugh Gwynn commanded the snow *Ruby* and annually made several voyages to the West Indies. These voyages officially began and ended at the colony's official ports of Urbanna, Accomac, Yorktown and Norfolk. Hugh preferred Accomac, directly across the Bay from Gwynn's Island. In 1749, Hugh built and launched the large brig *Betty and Jenny* on Milford Haven. This one-hundred-ton brig was the largest yet built on the island. Her completion took many months, and, in the fall of 1750, Hugh registered her in Williamsburg. Like the *Ruby*, the *Betty and Jenny* served in the West Indies trade. From Barbados, Antigua, and Jamaica Hugh brought back rum, sugar, limes, oranges, valuable spices and other highly profitable goods. Some of these West Indies' goods graced Gwynn's Island tables.[11]

Gwynn's Island residents lived comfortably. A deed from 1754 shows three island houses which are typical colonial story and a half houses with brick chimneys. The second floor of each house had dormer windows. These are remodeled versions of the island's earliest houses with raised floors, glass windows, plastered interior walls and decorative paint, trim and architectural features. The furnishings of the Gwynns, Keebles, Reades and Brooks houses reflected a modest level of affluence.[12]

At the outbreak of the Seven Years War in 1756, young Walter Gwynn purchased the thirty-ton sloop *Friendship*. This was his first investment in shipping, and he chose his friend and kinsman Robert Tompkins to command the *Friendship*. Wartime made the West Indies trade highly profitable but very risky. Nonetheless, this venture began a successful and prosperous business relationship for both Gwynn and Tompkins. Hugh Gwynn followed the trend to small, fast vessels in the trade. In 1759, he commanded a small, two-masted schooner captured earlier by the British. Hugh renamed his vessel for members of his family—*Betsey and Peggy*.[13]

With the advent of peace in 1763, Hugh took a less active role in maritime affairs, the church, and his community. Walter and John Gwynn assumed responsibility for most voyages to the Indies. Hugh used his extensive maritime experience and helped Humphrey Keeble design and build the schooner *James* on the island in 1766. Until the *James*, Gwynn's Island families preferred square rigged vessels such as the sloop and the brig for overseas commerce.[14]

The sloop was the standard West Indies colonial trader during the first half of the early eighteenth century. By the 1760s, schooners such as the *James* appeared more frequently in the trade. The schooner was about the same hull length as the sloop, but it had a two-masted rig which required only half the crew of a single-masted sloop. The fore-and-aft schooner rig improved a vessel's sailing characteristics in the more confined waters of both the Bay and the Indies. The schooner's sail area, spread on two shorter masts rather than one tall mast, lowered the vessel's center of gravity and permitted a shallower draft. Shallow draft vessels gained advantages in both access and maneuver in Tidewater as well as the Indies. To compensate for the shallower draft, schooners grew in breadth (beam) in order to accommodate the cargo volume of the sloops. The schooner's physical characteristics produced a fast sailing vessel which required only a small crew. Faster vessels meant shorter voyages for perishable cargoes. Shorter voyages also meant more voyages annually. By the end of the eighteenth century, the schooner replaced the sloop as an overseas trader. With few exceptions. almost all vessels built at Gwynn's Island after 1766 were schooners such as Humphrey Keeble's *James*.[15]

In 1768, John and Walter Gwynn built the twenty-ton schooner *Endeavor*. John became the master or captain while Walter held majority ownership. The *Endeavor* served the Gwynns in the Indies trade until the American Revolution, and its success increased John's wealth. He bought the sloop *Baltimore Packet* in 1769 and hired Ebeneezer Coombes as master. Coombes continued to command John's vessels through the Revolution. Only one or two successful voyages a year was sufficient to maintain the island residents' comfortable lifestyle.[16]

Natural disasters occasionally disrupted life on Gwynn's Island. In October 1749, a huge hurricane swept away or damaged many canoes and small vessels. The storm delayed completion of Hugh Gwynn's big vessel *Betty and Jenny*. Damage to the island's homes and buildings diverted resources needed to complete the vessel. In September 1766, a smaller hurricane caused moderate damage to the region. In September 1769, a much larger hurricane struck the entire east coast. All the British colonies from Georgia to Massachusetts suffered great damage. This hurricane destroyed homes, vessels and crops, drowned livestock and people, and caused much suffering in Tidewater Virginia. Gwynn's Island suffered some damage. However, near the island's southeast shore, the hurricane provided drama for local residents. The hurricane caused another disaster just off the island.[17]

The two-masted snow *Fortune* entered the Chesapeake Bay from London late on September 7, 1769, just as the hurricane arrived from the South. The *Fortune* carried about seventy crew and passengers, including fifty-seven indentured servants destined for Annapolis. Captain Roundtree of the *Fortune* decided to continue northward up the Bay and hopefully outrun the hurricane. The hurricane moved faster than the *Fortune*, and the increasing winds carried away the vessel's masts and rigging. In the dark, wind and rain the crew cut away the vessel's two masts and anchored off Gwynn's Island. The *Fortune* rode the hurricane into the early morning of September 8. At the height of the hurricane, just before dawn, the anchor failed, and the vessel was driven ashore near White's Creek just south of the island. The indentured servants and some of the crew jumped overboard in the surf and disappeared into the woods.[18]

The *Fortune*'s voyage from London had been unusually long. During the voyage, she was forced to hail passing vessels and from these the *Fortune* purchased, begged or borrowed fresh water and provisions. Her weakened crew and starved passengers influenced Capt. Roundtree's decision to try to outrun the hurricane to Annapolis. After the *Fortune* washed ashore, the prospect of freedom and safety overwhelmed the snow's crew and passengers. Some who escaped were sailors and farmers, but others listed their professions as carpenters, carvers, weavers, wood turners, wheelwrights, tailors and even a surgeon. Generous rewards for their capture and "expenses for their (captor's) troubles" found few bounty hunters, though posted at George Brian's tavern nearby and as far away as the Swan Tavern in Yorktown.

Henry Knight of Kingston Parish in Gloucester County corresponded with the *Fortune*'s owners. In the spring of 1770, Knight auctioned the *Fortune*'s fixtures and remaining salvageable equipment. The stripped hull remained aground near the east end of the island.

Shortly after the demise of the *Fortune*, personal tragedy struck the family of Humphrey and Frances Gwynn. On September 12, 1770, their fifteen year old son, John, drowned in a boating accident on Milford Haven. Six months later, Humphrey and Frances' infant daughter, Lucy, died only a month after her baptism. The parish, island community and families felt these losses deeply.[19]

In 1772 Walter Gwynn built the schooner *Lively* in 1772 and entered her in the Indies trade. However, tensions with Great Britain and the problems in Boston affected shipbuilding on the island. The Virginia colony embargoed many English products in 1773, including tea. The embargo impacted island trade. Virginia initiated local "Committees of Safety" to oversee the embargo as well as protect merchant interests. The Committee had oversight of all goods brought into the county, and, as prominent traders, the island residents carefully assessed the barometer of popular feeling. The Gwynns and Keebles did not actively participate in the Gloucester County Committee of Safety. Nonetheless, they remained stanch friends as well as kinsmen of several members of the Committee. The island families generally adhered to the embargo.

In November of 1774, the Gloucester Committee of Safety learned of a serious violation of the embargo at Yorktown. Merchant John Norton had allowed Captain Howard Esten to import tea into the colony on his ship *Virginia*. While the Gloucester Committee met and voted to destroy the tea, the York Committee of Safety boarded the *Virginia* and threw the tea into the York River. The Gloucester committee arrived in time to witness the tea's destruction. The "Yorktown Tea Party" incident remained a topic of discussion well into 1775. It hardened the patriotic resolve of local merchants and Gwynn's Island residents.[20]

After Governor Dunmore abandoned Williamsburg in June 1775 and moved to Hampton Roads, loyalists joined his fleet. Few loyalists went from Gloucester County, and fewer still from Kingston Parish. None on the island left. The necessity to "take sides" and the presence of Dunmore's hostile fleet in Hampton Roads disrupted trade and business alliances. Many of Dunmore's loyalists represented both the merchant community in Virginia and large firms with strong British connections. Business in Hampton Roads suffered, and merchants left the area to continue their enterprises. Kingston Parish attracted some of these businessmen. The parish was already a prominent shipbuilding area, and vessels moved goods. Dunmore's actions halted the collection of duties and the regulated maritime trade, but the suspension of regulations accompanied a sharp increase in vessel seizures, particularly by Dunmore's loyalists. A demand for vessels rapidly developed. The island completed its vessels under construction and found ready buyers. Dunmore also increased raiding activities, and, though the island was a vulnerable target, no British or loyalists attacked the island. However, on nearby Queen's Creek, opposite the island's west end, lived John Wilkie. Wilkie had emigrated to Kingston Parish from Scotland several years earlier, established a local shipyard, and conducted business with the West Indies. In April 1776, the Gloucester Committee of Safety arrested and tried Wilkie as a loyalist actively supporting Dunmore. After a bitter trial Wilkie was exiled and his property condemned, including several vessels. Within a month, Wilkie had escaped and joined Dunmore's fleet as master of the schooner *Lady Gower*.[21]

In order to curb Dunmore's raids and discourage loyalist activity, Virginia stationed troops at strategic points on the Chesapeake. Gloucester militia Captain Robert Mathews and a small guard unit operated from Gwynn's Island. They used the island's log canoes to patrol the mouth of the Piankatank River. Duty on the island was pleasant, the islanders most hospitable, the water "sweet" and the food plentiful. The Virginia Convention recognized Mathews' efforts and authorized pay for the captain and his men on May 15, 1775. But little rain fell in May, and the island's cattle, sheep and horses crowded the island's wells and springs. Most of Capt. Mathews' guard lived in Kingston Parish and went home frequently. Besides the weather, Dunmore's huge fleet in Hampton Roads provided conversation and speculation to pass the time. Rumors reached the island that the fleet had prepared to sail. Annapolis, Philadelphia, New York or one of the southern Colonies seemed likely destinations. No one on Gwynn's Island imagined that the fleet intended to occupy their small island.[22]

Loyalist Exodus

In the early evening of Thursday, May 16, His Majesty's Ship *Roebuck*, 44 guns, Captain Andrew S. Hamond, sighted the pilot boat *Dolphin* off the coast of Virginia. Master Edward James recognized the *Roebuck* and her escort vessels. Signals were exchanged, sails lowered, and James went aboard the *Roebuck* with Dunmore's letter. On board the *Roebuck*, James was led below to the Captain's cabin. Hamond politely received James, offered him a glass of wine and sat down with Dunmore's letter. Dunmore stressed his need for naval support as the rebels gathered strength and boldness. His position grew more perilous daily. Hamond decided to alter his course from the Carolinas to Virginia. He wrote a brief note to Dunmore, thanked James and summoned the *Roebuck*'s officers. Shortly after James returned to the *Dolphin*, the *Roebuck* and her escorts made sail for Hampton Roads.[1]

The next morning, while underway, Hamond decided to gather some fresh provisions. He sent his tenders *Pembroke* and schooner *Ranger* to the nearby Virginia coast. Accompanied by the *Dolphin* the raiding party sailed through Chincoteague inlet and anchored off Wallop's Island. Forty armed seamen from the British vessels went ashore and ordered the island's tenants to corral their cattle. The British offered to pay for these and other provisions. They also told the islanders that resistance to their demands would bring retaliation. The islanders moved slowly, and the British grew anxious about possible militia attacks. The British quickly killed and butchered the first six cattle. Two other cattle were tied up, and all then removed to the nearby vessels. The British paid no compensation to the islanders. As the British sailed away, they exchanged shots with the islanders. No casualties resulted and the tenders rejoined the *Roebuck*.[2]

On Sunday morning, May 19, Hamond's fleet anchored in the Elizabeth River. Hamond went on board the *Dunmore* and met with Governor Dunmore. News of the *Roebuck*'s arrival in Virginia had preceded him and gave Dunmore time to prepare for what would be an important meeting. After the formalities of introducing officers, sharing wine and exchanging pleasantries, Dunmore informed Hamond of two major problems. Informants had told Dunmore that the rebels had sent cannon to Norfolk. The arrival of cannon threatened both the British fleet and their fortifications at Tucker's Point. In addition, the rebels had gathered fireships to be sent among Dunmore's crowded wooden fleet.[3]

Dunmore's other problem was disease. Some of Dunmore's Royal Ethiopians had small pox. Consultation with the *Roebuck*'s surgeon confirmed Dunmore's advisers—everyone must be inoculated. Even with inoculations, the British forces could suffer significant losses. Inoculation appeared rational to Dunmore, Hamond and their advisers, but many in the floating town were local Virginians. In 1768 riots had broken out in Norfolk over the inoculation issue. Many residents saw the inoculation process as a sinister plot to spread, not halt, the disease. The controversy had subsided but not died. In 1776, inoculation offered hope but was not infallible. Even with inoculations, given the close confined conditions in the vessels of Dunmore's floating town, containment of smallpox or any disease would be almost impossible.[4]

The meeting between Hamond, Dunmore and their advisers lasted well into the afternoon. They finally decided to move troops, ships and loyalists from Hampton Roads. Hamond's arrival and consultation ended Dunmore's occupation of Hampton Roads. Hamond recognized the increasingly untenable strategic position of Dunmore's huge, poorly defended fleet, the crowded anchorage, and the camp on Tucker's Point. Cannon placed along the Elizabeth River, twelve- or eighteen-pounders, could easily bombard the fleet. Cannon placed at the mouth of the Elizabeth River could "bottle up" the fleet in the river. The majority of the over one hundred vessels in the fleet contained loyalist non-combatants. Hamond advised Dunmore that these noncombatants represented a major drain on his limited resources and a danger if fighting broke out.[5]

Hamond saw the noncombatant loyalists as a serious liability and he recommended that Dunmore send them to St. Augustine, New York or back to England. Dunmore saw the loyalist presence less rationally. These loyalists were Dunmore's supporters, constituents, allies and fellow exiles, some for almost a year. Dunmore was their governor, representing and appointed by King George III. Dunmore was also, nominally, a vice-admiral. This prerogative of Royal Governors provided Dunmore with the power over Virginia's waters and jurisdiction in Admiralty Courts to decide related naval matters. Captain Hamond could recommend and perhaps persuade the governor but he could not order Dunmore to divest himself of non-combatants. Nonetheless, Hamond had accomplished the decision to move the fleet from Hampton Roads. That Sunday night he prepared orders to his lieutenants, the other naval vessels and the marines on shore. As soon as possible, they would depart Hampton Roads. Their destination was undetermined.[6]

Following the decision to move his fleet, Dunmore needed to evaluate all options. For some time Dunmore's supporters had recommended other sites from which to carry on his military campaign. Dunmore needed to obtain defensible shore facilities, water, provisions and a deep anchorage. Few locations in Virginia satisfied those needs. Hamond, Dunmore and others discussed several alternatives at that Sunday meeting. Gwynn's Island was one of these alternate locations for the fleet, but no decision was reached. Regardless of the destination, the decision to leave Hampton Roads brought forth a number of immediate problems. Foremost was the fleet's condition.

The decision to leave Hampton Roads required enormous preparations in the fleet. Most of the over one hundred vessels could not sail without some effort to repair rigging, mend sails and clean vessel bottoms of marine growth. Some required major work to be seaworthy. A few vessels were completely unseaworthy and were abandoned or destroyed. All the vessels needed provisions

Figure 4 Floating Town Vessels

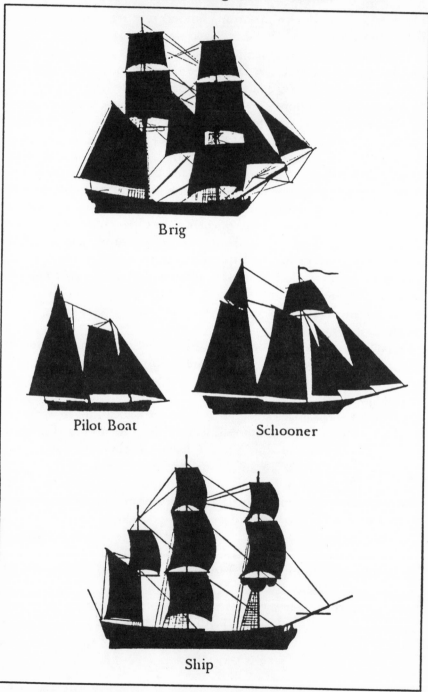

Brig

Pilot Boat

Schooner

Ship

Figure 5 Floating Town Vessels

Snow

Sloop

Sloop

Frigate

and water. Many needed crews. The two loyalist regiments, British regulars, sailors, marines and civilians had to be re-embarked on their vessels. Reboarding those forces and resupply of the vessels, combined with the destruction of unsalvageable vessels, necessitated further hard decisions. Some of the civilians aboard the condemned vessels had to be moved, and no room remained for much of their meager belongings. Leaving Hampton Roads required considerable effort, during which time the British would be even more vulnerable to patriot attack.

On Tuesday, May 21, some military units and civilians at Tucker's Point, including the spouses of the Royal Ethiopians, began to board the vessels. Fair weather and calm waters made the numerous boat trips between shore and the vessels easier. However, most of the loyalist vessels lacked trained seamen, and this slowed preparations. On Wednesday, the *Otter* and *Roebuck*'s seamen helped with the re-embarkation. Some navy seamen remained to help crew the vessels. The *Otter*'s crew also brought down three schooners and a sloop which were in poor condition. They grounded these vessels on the flats off Craney Island, cut away their masts, removed all usable gear, and chopped holes through their hulls below the waterlines. That afternoon the military units stationed at the Tucker's Point fortifications withdrew to the transports. The *Fowey*'s and *Dunmore*'s guns covered the operation and remained nearby to prevent interference by the patriots. Some of the seaworthy vessels began to move down the Elizabeth River into Hampton Roads where the *Roebuck* awaited them. From the steeple of St. John's Church in Hampton, militia Major James Hendrick recorded in detail the vessel movements. That night he sent his observations to General Andrew Lewis in Williamsburg.[7]

At dawn on Thursday, the *Otter* moved to the mouth of the western branch of the Elizabeth River and anchored just before 9 a.m. Shortly afterward, two small, unidentified vessels sailed close to the *Otter*, and Captain Montague fired two main deck guns at them as a warning to keep their distance. Later that day, the remaining loyalist vessels moved down the Elizabeth River toward a rendezvous in Hampton Roads. By late Thursday afternoon, Tucker's Point was completely evacuated. Marines and seamen from the *Fowey*, acting on Dunmore's orders, destroyed the houses, bakeries, distilleries and all other buildings at the Point. Some were dismantled and others burned. Fresh breezes fanned the flames. In addition the British destroyed almost 45,000 precious bushels of salt for which no space in the fleet existed. By 6 p.m. the *Fowey* and the *Dunmore* anchored in Hampton Roads. Those breezes generally helped the operation but caused problems for a few. Five loyalist vessels, with shorthanded and unskilled crews, ran aground. In the failing light, the *Otter* moved near the grounded vessels to protect them.[8]

Friday, May 24, began with fog. The *Otter* spent the early morning freeing the five vessels which had grounded the day before. These and other stragglers eventually moved into Hampton Roads. Hamond, Dunmore and the other naval officers carefully surveyed abandoned Tucker's Point, assessed the fleet's readiness, and mustered all hands. By 5 p.m. the fleet was reassembled in Hampton Roads. With the fleet in readiness, Hamond and Dunmore addressed the question of their destination.[9]

At Tucker's Point, the retreating marines and seamen deliberately let bystanders, including patriots, overhear that their anticipated voyage was to Halifax, Nova Scotia. That same information was forwarded by the patriots to Williamsburg. In truth, the fleet did not intend to leave the Chesapeake nor did the patriots believe the rumors. The decision where to relocate belonged to Dunmore. He considered Yorktown, Urbanna, Gwynn's Island and the Eastern Shore. These destinations had been discussed for some time prior to Hamond's arrival. Since the previous Sunday, when the decision to sail was made, Dunmore had weighed this question carefully. Gradually, he reached his decision.[10]

Two persons certainly influenced Dunmore. They were Andrew Sprowl of Portsmouth and John Grymes of Middlesex County. Sprowl's long association with mariners favored the rural areas of the Bay where shipbuilding sites, naval stores and food supplies were abundant. Many such sites existed on the Middle Peninsula—particularly Gloucester County. Before the Revolution, this county produced many vessels, from the smallest to the largest. The destruction of Norfolk drove shipbuilding talent to this as well as other areas. Gloucester County, particularly its

Kingston Parish, had a huge coastline of hundreds of miles. On its northern edge was a large, sparsely inhabited island—Gwynn's Island. Sprowl knew the island as did John Grymes. John Grymes and his family also knew Dunmore well. Grymes held high offices under Dunmore, and their families knew each other socially. Dunmore often spent his summers at Rosegill Plantation near the Grymes' estate in Middlesex County. Middlesex County was directly across the Piankatank River from Gloucester County and Gwynn's Island. Grymes also recommended Gwynn's Island for strategic as well as selfish reasons. Grymes assumed his presence would draw loyalists from Middlesex County and he could better protect his own property if nearby. From the information given him, Hamond concluded "that it [Gwynn's Island] formed an excellent Harbor, had plenty of fresh water, and could most easily be defended from the Enemy" as well as being "inhabited by many Friends of Government." All agreed to move the fleet to Gwynn's Island once the wind turned favorable.[11]

In Maryland, the Colony's convention met to discuss the actions of their Governor, Robert Eden. Correspondence from the British Government to Eden had fallen into patriot hands. It revealed the possibility that Eden might assist, by force, the return of conservative British rule in Maryland. The Convention's resolution of May 24 politely refrained from any accusations against Eden. But the Convention did "require that he (Eden) leave this province, and that he is at full liberty to depart peaceably with his effects." The Convention also referenced Dunmore in its resolution. Eden immediately made arrangements to get in touch with Virginia's governor. The Convention allowed the schooner *Friendship* to sail south with Eden's secretary, Mr. Robert Smith, to locate the *Fowey* and Captain Montague. Eden was unaware of the *Roebuck*'s arrival and the subsequent preparations to leave Hampton Roads.[12]

At 8:30 a.m. on Saturday, May 25, with the entire fleet finally assembled, Hamond signalled the naval vessels from the *Roebuck*. Despite the crowded harbor, confused situation and haze, the *Otter* correctly read and acknowledged the *Roebuck*'s signal from three miles away. Confident that his communications were secure, Hamond prepared the order of sailing while he waited for the high tide that afternoon. Hamond flew the broad blue pennant of a commodore. He was a captain in the Royal Navy but Dunmore requested Hamond assume the rank of commodore due to the large number of vessels under his command. The prerogative belonged to Governor Dunmore to authorize that action and to Captain Hamond to assume it. He did. At 4 p.m., Commodore Hamond made the signal to sail. The *Fowey* led the front or van of the squadron, now under Hamond's complete authority. The loyalist vessels maneuvered into a crescent-shaped anchorage in Lynnhaven Bay with the *Roebuck* in the middle. The *Otter* brought up the rear of the squadron. Shortly after getting underway the *Otter* noticed a sloop in the fleet without sufficient sails and crew. At 5:30 p.m., a detachment from the *Otter* boarded the sloop, removed those on board and set fire to the vessel. Underway again by 6, the *Otter* made little progress. At 8:30 p.m., as darkness fell, the *Otter* anchored off Old Point Comfort. All the vessels maintained strict watches that night, lest the rebels should raid from shore. From the quarterdeck of the *Otter* the fires of a militia camp could be seen on Old Point Comfort, barely 1,000 yards distant. Along Lynnhaven Bay mounted patriot horsemen patrolled the shoreline. They belonged to Captain Lemuel Cornick's troop of Virginia Light Horse. Guard boats from the *Roebuck* and *Fowey* rowed between the fleet and shoreline throughout the night. In the remains of Norfolk, Portsmouth and Hampton, no one celebrated. Unaware of Dunmore's plans, they wondered what Sunday would bring.[13]

By 8 a.m. on Sunday, May 26, the entire fleet set sail for Gwynn's Island—about thirty nautical miles from Lynnhaven Bay. The wind was moderate, from the southwest and the weather warm and hazy. The voyage was slow and uneventful. One hundred vessels of all sizes, rigs, and conditions of seaworthiness, loaded to capacity and manned by seamen of widely differing skills safely reached Gwynn's Island that same day. The *Roebuck* anchored first in the Bay above Wolf Trap Shoals. The rest of the vessels sailed under her guns and anchored in Hill's Bay, in the mouth of the Piankatank River. The last vessels sailed past the *Roebuck* in the early evening. With all vessels safely anchored, the *Roebuck* shifted her anchorage to defend the channel between Stove Point in Middlesex County and Cherry Point on Gwynn's Island.[14]

On the island, the small militia guard under Captain Mathews quickly retreated to the mainland and sent riders to the Gloucester County Courthouse and Williamsburg. Local residents watched the fleet arrive and anchor. They assumed that the fleet might be in the vicinity for several days. Clearly, the British would land and seize provisions as, in the past, ships and large convoys had often rendezvoused at Gwynn's Island before sailing elsewhere. The enormous size of this fleet struck awe in the patriots. Militia units in York, Gloucester, Middlesex, Lancaster, Northumberland and other counties spread the alarm. Many citizens of Gloucester, especially Kingston Parish, gathered out of sight along the shoreline to get a glimpse of the largest fleet they had ever seen. It was also the largest hostile fleet to ever sail in the Chesapeake Bay, before or since.

As darkness fell, Hamond reconnoitered the island. Accompanied by John Grymes and the Maryland loyalist William Parker, Hamond had a boat crew row along the island's shores. He took soundings along the shore and evaluated the inlets and creeks to determine the best site for a landing in force. Hamond's party then returned aboard the *Dunmore* with their findings.[15]

While the local residents went to bed, Hamond and Dunmore worked well past midnight. They prepared the order of battle for an amphibious assault on the island. Marines, soldiers and loyalists checked and prepared their arms and equipment. Seamen prepared and outfitted the dozens of boats needed to carry the force ashore. Stiff resistance was not anticipated but also could not be discounted. Hamond wanted a quick assault in force. The over-crowded conditions of the vessels made it imperative to get people ashore where they could get light, water, and fresh air. The severe shortage of supplies made fresh meat and vegetables very important. The spread of disease made it imperative to place some distance between the sick and infected persons and the fleet. Hamond and Dunmore ordered a pre-dawn invasion of Gwynn's Island. In the early morning of May 27 all was ready.[16]

British Invasion

At 4 a.m. on Monday, May 27, one hundred Royal Marines from the *Roebuck*, *Fowey*, and *Otter*, landed on Gwynn's Island. Rowed by sailors in eight large boats, they landed simultaneously in the middle of the island's western shore. Hamond and Dunmore watched from their quarterdecks for any signs of opposition or flashes of gunfire. The gun crews on the naval vessels were ready to provide covering fire should a retreat prove necessary. The marines met no resistance. They moved from the beach up a short slope to the tree line. There they established a base and sent out pickets to detect and deter a counterattack.[1]

At dawn, elements of the 14th Regiment, Dunmore's Royal Ethiopians, the Queen's Own Loyal Virginians, and armed Royal Navy seamen went ashore in several waves. This brought the total British forces ashore to approximately 700 men. While the marines held the landing site and guarded the boats, parties from the 14th, Royals and Queens marched along the north and south shore of the island to the eastern end. They returned in about two hours and rejoined the other units. The British forces established a camp at the southwest end of the island, closest to the mainland. There, the deep but narrow channel measured barely two hundred yards across. It was the most likely place for a patriot attack from the mainland. Before 8 a.m. patriot militia on the mainland opened a sporadic fire on the British forces building the camp.[2]

By mid-morning, the patriot small-arms fire threatened to stop work on the camp, largely the task of the Ethiopians. The

Otter and two tenders moved their anchorage to the "Narrows," the deep channel between the island and the mainland. The *Otter* and tenders returned fire at the mainland, their large caliber cannon intimidating the patriots. Unable to effectively return the cannonade the patriots ceased fire and contented themselves with observation. Work on the British camp and fortifications continued. Near the landing site, a shore party began to dig a deep well for use of the British.

After the island was secure the British advised the island's residents to gather their personal possessions and leave the island. The Keebles' house at Cherry Point became an observation post to watch the fleet and the landing site. The Reade residence on the north shore became the seat of John Grymes' "plantation." Once ashore, Grymes quickly confiscated the island's horses and established a troop of cavalry. He stationed his cavalry in the middle of the island and used the Reade house as his headquarters. Dunmore found the arrangement advantageous since Grymes could send his horsemen within minutes to any part of the island. The Gwynn and Reade homes on the Haven became headquarters for the British regimental officers. The Keebles, Reades, and Gwynns reluctantly moved to the mainland. A few residents remained to ensure fair treatment of their property.[3]

One significant asset on the island was almost immediately put to use. The British found over five hundred cattle, sheep and hogs, plus hundreds of chickens and other domesticated animals. The British used their gold—backed by the threat of force—to acquire these animals. Some of the loyalists in the fleet had enjoyed no fresh meat for almost two months and their poor diet undoubtedly facilitated the spread of disease. So abundant were the island's food resources that Dunmore soon shipped fresh supplies to British Governor Patrick Tonyn in West Florida. The British now regretted the tremendous quantity of salt dumped in the Elizabeth River during the evacuation. Shortages of salt to preserve meat and casks to store the meat developed on the island. Within days water on the island also became a problem. The few springs and dug wells on the island had usually been sufficient for the islanders and the needs of passing vessels. The island seldom supported more than a hundred residents. Now almost thirty times that number demanded water daily. As summer neared the water levels dropped further. The well begun by the British near the landing site eventually proved the only constant water supply, but its output was limited.[4]

In addition to the camp on the southwest end of the island, Dunmore ordered Major Byrd of the Ethiopians to build several redoubts for defense of the island's south shore, opposite the mainland. Byrd began construction the day of the landings. One site, called Fort Hamond, defended the camp from attack across the Narrows. The second and third sites chosen were on high ground near the Gwynn residences. The last site was between a Gwynn residence and Sandy Point. Byrd used all available Ethiopians who were fit to work. Each redoubt mounted two cannon on field carriages. The redoubts took over a week to complete.[5]

The occupation's first day pleased Dunmore. No casualties had resulted from the landing. British troops controlled the entire island, worked on construction of a large encampment and built defensive fortifications. The camp and fortifications had covering fire from the *Otter* and other naval vessels which also suppressed the harassing sniper fire from the patriots. No significant patriot counterattack appeared to be forming. Several small British vessels patrolled Milford Haven to prevent any patriot raid from the mainland. Grymes' cavalry troop could rapidly prevent an insurrection or respond to an attack. The anchorage was secure, guarded by the *Roebuck*. A permanent water supply was under construction while enough water existed on the island to satisfy immediate needs. The residents had offered no resistance and the few that remained were coerced into reluctant cooperation. The food and animals found on the island surpassed expectations. It not only satisfied immediate needs but would provide a month's fresh provisions.

The island's only apparent weakness as a base of operation was the distance between it and the mainland. A considerable force of patriots, with cannon and small craft, might successfully attack the island. Still, Dunmore characteristically played down the ability of the patriots to organize and mount an offensive before his own preparations were completed. Dunmore had found many loyalists in Hampton Roads. The reports of Sprowl and Grymes indicated the same would be true in the areas near the island. Dunmore

Figure 6 Invasion of Gwynn's Island

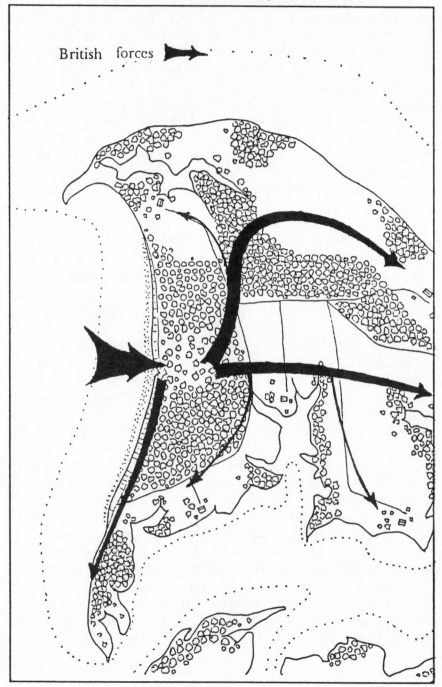

British   forces

anticipated loyalist support from the mainland. The patriots who fired on his encampment represented a fringe element, or so Dunmore assumed. He believed once loyal Virginians knew he had a new base of operations, they would flock to the King's standard. Dunmore would need them. Some of the troops who came ashore that day had already died or were dying of disease. Fresh air, water, food and shore life had not checked the diseases.

Hamond, like Dunmore, was also pleased with the first day's operation. He, too, was worried about the "Narrows." It would require both additional fortification and increased guards which could only be drawn from limited resources. Hamond disliked the use of his marines to reinforce Dunmore's sickly soldiers. The seasoned British naval commander saw that many of Dunmore's troops sent ashore were unfit for duty, and more showed signs of illness.[6]

An incident with mixed blessings occurred the second night off Gwynn's Island. Three African Americans in a log canoe from the near shore hailed the *Roebuck*. Second Lieutenant William South invited them aboard and warmly welcomed them with greetings and handshakes. First Lieutenant Robert Smith advised Hamond of visitors and brought them to Hamond's cabin. The Commodore put them at ease and suggested that they and others who joined the British would be "well used." Hamond also asked about local militia forces, and he was told none were closer than six miles. He also questioned his visitors about cattle and the possibility of getting them from the mainland without opposition. They assured Hamond that many cattle were available and little risk existed. More to the point, Hamond asked if they could get fowl and sheep that night for the *Roebuck*'s officers. He assured them of good pay for their efforts and that eventually, when the war was over, they would have their freedom and their own plantations. Reassured by Hamond's offer and manner, one of the trio returned to the canoe alongside the *Roebuck*. He came back to the Commodore's cabin with chickens, ducks and geese as well as his wife, two children, and another African-American male adult.[7]

Hamond recorded nothing of this incident, but William Barry, an American prisoner on the *Roebuck*, overheard the entire exchange. The log canoe was tied near a gun port where Barry was detained. When the last occupants of the canoe left, Barry saw

his chance "to make his escape or die in the attempt." He slipped
into the canoe, cut the canoe's painter (rope) to the*Roebuck* and let
the canoe drift astern. The incoming tide carried Barry and the
canoe up the Piankatank. At daybreak, he paddled ashore to the
mainland of Middlesex County. He met a resident who warned
Barry that, if found, he might be turned over to the British.
Unshaven, unclean, unkempt but undaunted, Barry pressed on to
a reported camp of patriots. He found the camp and advised
militia Colonel John Churchill of the British plans to raid for cattle
and other provisions. Churchill immediately sent forty horsemen
to drive all livestock from the shoreline to the county's interior
above Urbanna. Eventually, Barry made his way back to
Philadelphia. Hamond also made no mention of Barry's escape,
but the *Roebuck*'s officers probably enjoyed the fowl and drank to
their successful occupation of Gwynn's Island.[8]

With the island secure, Hamond turned his attention to
exclusively naval problems. On Tuesday morning, May 28,
Hamond prepared orders for Captain Squires of the *Otter*. He
ordered Squires to take the *Otter* and two tenders and cruise for
two weeks at the mouth of the Chesapeake Bay. Squires was to
advise incoming vessels of the relocation of Dunmore's floating
town and to seek a brig Dunmore anxiously anticipated. That
afternoon, Captain James Nicholson in the Maryland State Navy
frigate *Defence* spotted large warships off Windmill Point, including
the *Roebuck* with Hamond's broad blue (Commodore's) pennant.
The *Defence* had cruised south to protect Maryland's shipping as
well as that of Virginia. The fleet off Gwynn's Island told
Nicholson that Dunmore was on the move. No American vessel on
the Bay or combination of vessels could successfully oppose the
Roebuck. Nicholson wrote three letters on the 28th which advised
Maryland officials of the new developments. After remaining
overnight in Flood's Bay, Nicholson returned the next day to
Maryland waters.[9]

On the morning of the 29th, the snow *Santa Barbara* entered
the Bay. This Spanish packet boat originally carried four chests
containing 12,000 silver pesos for the Continental Congress and a
Spanish colonial official and informal emissary to the Congress,
Miguel Antonio Eduardo. HMS *Liverpool*, 28 guns, chased and
captured the *Santa Barbara* off Delaware Bay. Though technically

a neutral, the discovery of the silver stimulated the British to find ways to detain the Spanish packet boat. Agent Eduardo skillfully resisted the British efforts to compromise the neutrality and true mission of the *Santa Barbara*. In a further effort to uncover the *Santa Barbara*'s true mission, Captain Bellew of the *Liverpool* sent the captured vessel to Hamond in the Chesapeake. Bellew retained the chests of silver. In order to protect himself and his mission Eduardo kept a diary of this voyage and his experiences in British detainment.[10]

Soon after 10 a.m. the *Santa Barbara* was boarded by the *Otter* off the Virginia Capes and directed to Gwynn's Island. In mid-afternoon the *Santa Barbara*, accompanied by the *Dolphin* started up the Bay with the sea rising and the winds against them. They anchored at night and rode out the high seas. At noon on May 30, the weather moderated. Both vessels continued up the Bay and anchored next to the *Roebuck* in the early evening.[11]

Earlier that Thursday, the schooner *Friendship* arrived from Annapolis with Governor Eden's letters to Hamond and Dunmore. Hamond handled Eden's letter as he had earlier received Dunmore's on the *Dolphin*. He extended courtesies to Eden's secretary, Mr. Robert Smith, then he opened and carefully read Eden's letter. Eden needed Royal Navy assistance to leave Maryland. In short, the convention's ban of Eden and his appeal to the Royal Navy for help placed further major burdens on Hamond. Hamond wrote Eden that soon "one of the King's ships" would be sent for the Governor. Hamond's letter was both deferential and respectful. It brought Eden current with the situation in Virginia. Later, Hamond informed Dunmore of Eden's plight.[12]

After Secretary Smith's departure, Hamond sat down and wrote an even lengthier letter to Captain Bellew of the *Liverpool*. As with Eden, he brought Bellew current with the situation. He then assessed the Delaware River situation, discussed New York, current events in Maryland, and problems on the island. Hamond summarized his situation: "In short, I begin to find more employment for the *Roebuck* in Virginia than I expected."[13]

At this time, the once powerful Andrew Sprowl died on board his vessel in the floating town. Sprowl's experience and travels generally precluded a single disease such as smallpox being the cause of death. His age (62), weakened condition after months of shipboard confinement, shock at the loss of his shipyard, destruction of his fine home and other residential properties, and the prevalence of contaminated or spoiled food, bad water and disease in the floating town all certainly contributed to his death. He was buried on the island. He left behind a large family, and his widow went into mourning. Neither Hamond nor Dunmore recorded Sprowl's death.[14]

Friday, May 31 began with gale force winds. Early in the morning, Hamond sent a Lieutenant and some men to the *Santa Barbara*. He carefully searched the Spanish vessel's chests, lockers, compartments and other areas. The lieutenant then escorted Captain Gomalez and Mr. Eduardo, along with the ship's papers, to the *Roebuck*. Hamond questioned both Spaniards on their mission and "other matters." Satisfied for the moment, Hamond offered a pilot to take the *Santa Barbara* to an anchorage with the rest of the fleet. He also agreed to survey the Spanish vessel and determine her seaworthiness. The Spaniards accepted the offer and returned to their vessel. Hamond made notes of his interrogation and sent them to Dunmore. Next Hamond turned out the *Roebuck*'s crew and began preparations to exercise the ship under sail. Before he got underway, the *Otter* sailed into the anchorage with Dunmore's long-anticipated supply brig from Antigua. As the *Roebuck*'s crew drilled at anchor, Dunmore supervised the distribution of the brig's supplies.[15]

The first of June began early for the *Santa Barbara*. A British pilot arrived at 5 a.m. and took some effort to get the vessel underway. The Spanish vessel, hampered by the poor condition of her rigging, threaded her way carefully through the crowded anchorage to a spot near the *Dunmore*. Shortly after noon Captain Gomalez and Mr. Eduardo, with some of their best seamen, rowed to the *Dunmore*. The Governor politely received them, offered them wine, asked about their voyage, mission, and particularly the purpose of the silver. The Spaniards answered Dunmore's questions, carefully guarding the true destination of the silver. They also told the Governor of the poor condition of their vessel and rigging. Dunmore explained his role in the floating town and advised them that Hamond had jurisdiction in maritime matters. He also suggested, with some satisfaction, that the island defenses would be ready in a couple of days. Until then, the Spanish were not permitted ashore. In this way Dunmore kept them under virtual arrest, though neutrals.[16]

Hamond continued construction of the island's defenses. On the day of the invasion, he had stationed two tenders to patrol the Narrows and Milford Haven between the island and the mainland. He briefly reinforced the patrol with the *Otter*. Their presence discouraged raids by the patriots and intimidated snipers. But he needed a vessel better armed to permanently enforce the patrol. Hamond ordered cannon, tools to serve the cannon, boarding equipment, small arms, powder, shot and men for the schooner *Lady Charlotte*. Dunmore had commandeered this vessel earlier and used it as a tender. The cannon, Royal Navy Petty Officer, trained crew, and other equipment made the *Lady Charlotte* an integral and powerful unit in the island's defenses. Captain Montague of the *Fowey* supplied the equipment and men. Captain Squires of the *Otter* assigned his young nephew, Mr. Alexander Silver, to the *Lady Charlotte* as a midshipman. The *Lady Charlotte* was now a de facto Royal Navy vessel.[17]

June 2 was the first Sunday in several weeks that followed a normal routine. The Royal Navy vessels and most of the fleet held church services. After the services, a British naval tradition was the reading of the articles of war. The portion on "desertion" got particular emphasis. The proximity to shore, rural nature of the country, and risk of disease presented incentives and opportunities for desertion. The *Roebuck*'s men and others from the fleet deserted regularly. The patriots usually quarantined British deserters from the fleet. Disease had not been checked, even with the inoculations and treatment. The British ill and dying were quarantined at a camp on the eastern end of the island. Already, burials occurred daily.[18]

On Sunday, Eduardo hoisted the Spanish flag on the *Santa Barbara*. While not technically a British prize, he had been ordered by Hamond to keep the Spanish colors lowered. However, on Sundays Eduardo hoisted his country's flag "in the hope that those on land would realize we were Spanish." Eduardo saw Hamond on one of the transports and met with him, ostensibly to relate his conversation with the Governor. Eduardo's real concern was the silver which was to have been delivered to the Continental

Congress through the Philadelphia firm of Willing and Morris. That 12,000 pesos, and 500 more of his personal expense money, rested in the hold of HMS *Liverpool*. When Eduardo found Hamond, his "attitude did not make me feel very easy." Hamond informed Eduardo that shortly a decision would be made regarding disposition of the *Santa Barbara*.[19]

As promised, at 7 a.m. the next day, the *Roebuck*'s second lieutenant and the ship's carpenter, John Frost, went aboard the *Santa Barbara*. They surveyed the Spanish snow and examined her rigging. The officer suggested to Captain Gomalez and Mr. Eduardo that they prepare a defense for a Vice-admiralty Court which would decide the fate of the *Santa Barbara*. The trial would take place when the *Liverpool* arrived. The Spaniards had little interest in becoming British victims. Their country was not at war with Great Britain. Their detainment could be construed as piracy. Eduardo boldly challenged the lieutenant to return his weapons and he would prepare the packet boat for battle—"with the great expectation of being victorious." It was remarkable bravado by the Spaniards, but little more, since the Spaniard was anchored among a hundred British vessels. However, this defiance startled the lieutenant, who immediately ordered a new search of the vessel, looking for any weapons. The British even searched among the ballast stones in the foul-smelling and rat-infested bilges. Even though nothing was found, the lieutenant had the hatches to the hold sealed and seized the Captain's log. The carpenter finished his report, handed it to the Lieutenant and the British returned to the *Roebuck*.[20]

That morning the *Otter* returned to her station off the Virginia capes, and Hamond sent instructions to the *Fowey* regarding the King's birthday celebration the following day, June 4. The Commodore's instructions were followed. At noon on the 4th, the *Roebuck* began a 21-gun salute in honor of the King's Birthday. In accordance with instructions, the *Fowey* commenced her 21-gun salute on the second gun from the *Roebuck*. At least half a dozen tenders and the *Lady Charlotte* joined the celebration as well as the *Dunmore*. Even the guns at Fort Hamond saluted the King's birthday. The cannonade's noise carried for many miles across the waters.[21]

The next day "a gentleman in black from Somerset County

[Maryland] . . ." visited the Governor. The Eastern Shore of Maryland and Virginia contained strong loyalist sympathies. This first meeting between Dunmore and those persons representing the Eastern Shore loyalists greatly encouraged the Governor. He knew of the strong loyalist support there. Many loyalists who joined Dunmore from Hampton Roads had sent their families to the Eastern Shore during the troubles. Four of Maryland's Eastern Shore counties did not sign the Maryland Convention's notice for Governor Eden to quit the Colony. The relocation of Dunmore's floating town to Gwynn's Island greatly improved Eastern Shore loyalist access to Dunmore.[22]

Work on the British fortifications continued. All able bodied loyalists in the fleet contributed to the effort as the military units were under-strength due to fever and illness. Hamond refused to let his marines work on the fortifications, but grudgingly allowed them to do guard and sentry duty. The work concentrated on the southwest end of the island and its fortification. Fort Hamond was a redoubt with two cannon behind earthworks. It rose from the low, narrow peninsula and faced a large patriot battery on the opposite shore, approximately three hundred yards distant. Fort Hamond rose from land approximately five feet above sea level while the patriot redoubt was on an elevation of almost fifteen feet. This disparity at such close range exposed much of Fort Hamond and the British camp to patriot observation. Behind the British redoubt lay the main camp of the 14th Regiment, the Queen's Own Loyal Virginians and a few elements of Dunmore's Royal Ethiopians. At a narrow point on the peninsula, a ditch was cut from Milford Haven to Hill's Bay and the dirt made into an embankment on the camp side. This had the effect of making the entire southwest tip of the island into a fortified camp.[23]

On the southeastern tip of the island, two different projects progressed. At the extreme tip of the island a small redoubt was built to defend against raids or invasion from the shoreline opposite—Lower Windmill Point, now known as Point Breeze. Several low, marsh islands extended from the eastern mainland of the parish to Sandy Point on Gwynn's Island. A small force in boats could use these marsh islands to "leapfrog" over several narrow channels and attack Gwynn's Island. The British redoubt protected against this possibility. It also afforded protection to the quarantine camp established nearby. The other project in this area was the construction of a small, artificial harbor. A broad marsh extended south to the marsh islands and the mainland. The low-lying peninsula had many pines which blocked the fleet's view of the Bay. Dunmore and Hamond wanted to station a pilot boat nearby to provide notice of vessel movement on the Bay. A boat stationed on the Haven side of the Peninsula could serve several purposes. It could quickly sail through the Haven and warn the naval vessels to prepare a defense or sail to attack. A boat near Sandy Point could protect the redoubt as well as attack any enemy from the mainland arriving by water or across the marsh islands. But the Haven side of the peninsula had no deep harbor, even for a pilot boat with a draft of five to six feet. Accordingly, Hamond and Dunmore had a channel dug from the Haven to a large, deep pond on the peninsula. The channel measured thirty yards across, a hundred and fifty yards long and approximately six feet deep at low tide. The pond was large and deep enough to float a pilot boat approximately forty feet on deck. The labor came from the more able-bodied in the quarantine camp, troops in the nearby redoubt and commandeered slaves owned by the fleet's loyalist owners.

The patriots did not remain idle during the British construction. The militia forces on the mainland, with their high ground and screened by trees, initially required little defense. As their numbers grew and Virginia State forces under Colonel William Daingerfield arrived from Williamsburg, fortifications began. Under the direction of Continental Army engineer Major Stevens, the main redoubt was placed on the Narrows opposite Fort Hamond on the southwest peninsula. Another redoubt was begun to the east, intended for smaller cannon and to harass shipping and activity on the Haven. With the advantage of high ground, the patriots worked with better protection while they harassed the British efforts with relative ease. Patriot snipers repeatedly annoyed the British. Their fire killed no one but slowed completion of Fort Hamond and continually revealed the British vulnerability. Periodically, Hamond stationed the *Otter* and other smaller warships near the Narrows to discourage the snipers and reinforce the *Lady Charlotte* and her two tenders.

During the evening of June 6, three Americans, captured in

the Delaware a month before, escaped from the *Roebuck*. John Emmes, John Drury and Alexander Davis swam almost a mile to Middlesex County. When they eventually returned to Philadelphia, Emmes left a comprehensive account of his confinement. In addition to American prisoners, British sailors also deserted the fleet. Most were detained by the patriots, but some disappeared into the countryside. But the British experienced their worse losses from disease. Dunmore stated "there was not a ship in the fleet that did not throw one, two, or three or more dead overboard every night." These often washed ashore on the mainland and the patriots reported that often a dozen or more bodies came ashore daily. Those who died on the island were buried there. In some cases, the dead were buried in large graves which contained several individuals. The official British Navy sick list numbers rose as the weather turned warmer. While many sick were added daily, almost as many died.[24]

Both loyalist and African-American recruits also suffered losses. New recruits, which included escaped slaves and white loyalists, came forward daily to join Dunmore. The slaves came by canoe from Gloucester, Middlesex, York, Lancaster and Eastern Shore counties in Virginia and Maryland. Most of the loyalists came from the Eastern Shore counties and Delaware. Loyalist sympathies continued to run high on the Eastern Shore. Loyalists from Dunmore's fleet such as William Goodrich made almost weekly raids against known patriots on both the eastern and western Shores of the Bay. These raids encouraged loyalist support. The majority of these loyalists and slaves were males. They brought intelligence on patriot activities in their areas, news of supplies, vessel arrivals and departures, shipbuilding, patriot troop concentrations, and more loyalist support.[25]

Less than four miles from Gwynn's Island, the Virginia State Navy galley *Manly* was being completed on the East River in Kingston Parish. Captain Robert Tompkins spurred the builders to complete the galley. They needed little encouragement. On the Rappahannock, two other patriot galleys also neared completion. A British attack by water or land on the East River galley would have been dangerous. By mid-June over one thousand Continentals and militia awaited the British on the mainland, and the East River channel was too narrow and shallow for safe

Figure 7 Gwynn's Island Defenses

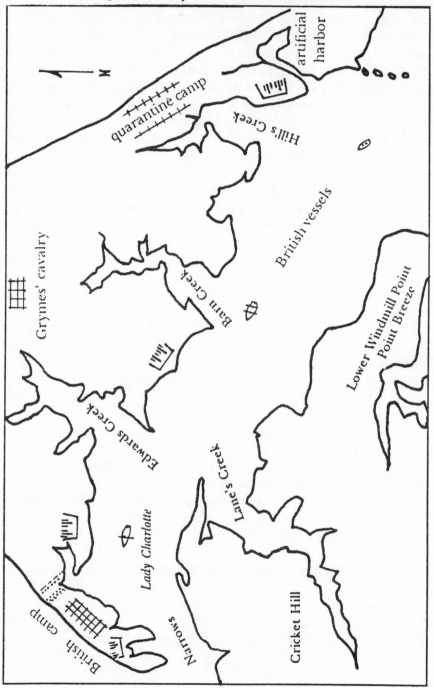

passage by the larger British warships. The Rappahannock River had none of these limitations. Goodrich, accompanied by several loyalist vessels, attempted to find the patriot galleys but failed. He contented himself with taking cattle, other livestock and some grain.[26]

On the Eastern Shore, Goodrich's attacks appeared more as military operations than hit-and-run raids. The Eastern Shore loyalists often backed, guided and participated with Goodrich in his attacks on patriot gatherings. In an attempt to discourage these raids the Virginia "Committee of Safety" authorized the pilot boat *Adventure* and her master, William Sanders, to cruise the Rappahannock and protect the inhabitants. Two days later, on Monday June 10, Hamond ordered William Goodrich in the *Lady Susan* and Lt. John Wright in the *Fincastle* to attack the galleys on the Rappahannock and a brig loading at Hobb's Hole, now Tappahannock.

The same day, Hamond sent a long and comprehensive letter to Sir Peter Parker. Parker commanded the Royal Navy forces on Clinton's southern expedition. Hamond's letter made a military appraisal of the island, their forces, needs and state of military preparedness. He observed to Parker, "I don't know a better place in Virginia for the headquarters of a fleet and an army." Hamond, though he wanted to join Parker's fleet, told him "I am unlikely to get clear of this encumbrance for some time." By "encumbrance" Hamond clearly meant his responsibility to Dunmore and the floating town.[27]

Hamond also wrote Captain Bellew of the *Liverpool* with instructions and suggestions. Hamond concluded that under new Admiralty rules, the *Santa Barbara* was a legitimate prize. Rather than try her in an Admiralty Court under Dunmore's Vice-Admiralty authority, Hamond suggested Bellew take her elsewhere for condemnation. Such an action would not reduce the navy's share of the prize money, but it could deprive Dunmore of a share of the proceeds. Condemnation by Dunmore might possibly be regarded as less legitimate than formal Admiralty proceedings. In either event, Hamond knew the Spanish would protest condemnation and sought the strongest case possible. Hamond sent the dispatches to Parker and Bellew in the tender *Ranger*, Edward James, Commander. By the *Ranger*, Hamond also sent a

supply of fresh beef, flour and other necessities for the British
garrison at St. Augustine.[28]

On June 11 one of the loyalist patrol vessels, a small sloop
with five men aboard, ran aground on the flats on the patriots'
side of the Narrows. Patriots quickly manned two log canoes and
set out from shore while other patriots fired at the loyalists.
Musket fire killed one of the loyalists and two others drowned
when they attempted to swim the "Narrows." The sloop yielded
brandy, rum, tools and some provisions. The patriots took these
back to their lines and consumed the brandy and rum "as the
water is very bad."[29]

The sloop's loss encouraged the patriots and further strained
the resources of the British. Hamond and Dunmore needed all
their vessels—particularly small, fast pilot boats as patrol and
dispatch vessels. Hamond's dispatch of the *Roebuck*'s tender with
letters and supplies limited his communications capability.
Hamond had not been in touch with the *Liverpool* for some weeks,
and he was anxious for word from her. The sloop lost in the
Narrows also had to replaced.

On Wednesday, Eduardo and Gomalez of the *Santa Barbara*
searched for the Governor. They needed his permission to repair
their vessel. Earlier, the *Roebuck*'s carpenter, John Frost, advised
the Spaniards that their mainmast boom must be replaced. Frost
would do the work, but the Governor had to give him permission
to cut down one of the island's trees to make the boom. Eduardo
and Gomalez found the Governor and Commodore on board a
small sloop similar to that lost the previous day. Hamond told the
Spaniards nothing should be done until the *Liverpool* arrived—
probably in two or three days. Hamond also invited the
disappointed Spaniards to dine with him aboard his flagship. They
agreed, but only apprehensively. They "did not wish to oppose
him [Hamond] in any way . . ."[30]

Dinner aboard HMS *Roebuck* was a formal affair. The huge
captain's cabin measured almost twenty by thirty feet. All the ships
officers attended, formally dressed. Wine preceded the meal, which
was served on china with silver tableware. On either side of the
cabin were large, eighteen-pound cannon which reminded guests
that despite the civilities, this was a ship of war. Hamond's
treatment of the Spaniards reflected his concern that no offense be

given neutrals. Hamond also correctly guessed that a record of his conduct and behavior would eventually be given to Eduardo's superiors, and possibly reviewed by senior foreign government officials as to its propriety. He wanted no charge of impropriety laid against him. That evening, Hamond impressed the Spaniards. Throughout their detention, the Spaniards both respected and feared the Commodore.[31]

The weather remained warm, fair and calm throughout June. The *Otter* returned from Hampton Roads on Friday evening, June 14th. She anchored near the *Roebuck*. Hamond sent 153 pounds of fresh beef aboard the *Otter* as the crew had been on salt rations. Hamond then stationed the *Otter* near the Narrows to prevent incidents such as the loss of the sloop.[32]

With the *Otter* back, Hamond decided to wait no longer for the *Liverpool*. Governor Eden's request had to be acknowledged. Accordingly, Hamond prepared orders for Captain Montague of the *Fowey* to escort Eden from Annapolis to Gwynn's Island. Hamond's orders gave Montague broad powers. Montague would travel under a flag of truce, "But if any insult whatever should be offered to either (Eden or Montague) you are at liberty to act against them (Marylanders) as you may think proper." Additionally, if Governor Eden was detained, then Montague was "to use your utmost endeavors to destroy the Town (Annapolis) and other ways distress the enemy by every means in your power." Hamond urged Montague use the "utmost expedition" on this mission. That left no time for negotiation or delay on Eden's part. The *Liverpool*'s continued absence weighed on Hamond's mind, and he only reluctantly dispatched the *Fowey* to Annapolis. On Sunday June 16, Hamond met with Montague. On board the *Roebuck*, Hamond stressed to Montague the delicacy and urgency of the *Fowey*'s mission. An eighteenth-century warship commander frequently exercised diplomacy. Hamond authorized Montague to use unrestricted force if diplomacy failed. Like Dunmore, Hamond was at war with the "rebels." Montague soon returned to the *Fowey* and prepared to get under way the next day.[33]

While Hamond and Montague met, Dunmore sent an invitation to Eduardo to dine with him that evening. Dunmore entertained Eduardo in the spacious stern cabin of the *Dunmore*. Eduardo knew few of the loyalists, but Dunmore assembled several to make the occasion sociable. John Grymes, Captain Leslie of the 14th and others probably attended as much for the opportunity to meet the Spaniard as to enjoy the Governor's cuisine and fine wines. Eduardo used the occasion to repeat his request for repairs to the *Santa Barbara*. Dunmore expressed his hope that Hamond would attend to the *Santa Barbara*'s needs. He also expressed his surprise at the *Liverpool*'s delay.[34]

Besieged

Early on the 17th, the *Fowey* sailed for Annapolis. The same day Catherine Sprowl, widow of the late Andrew Sprowl, applied to Hamond for permission to see her son, now held prisoner in North Carolina. The widow had spent the last two weeks mourning her husband's death. She wanted to see her oldest son, seek his counsel and share their grief. Hamond graciously complied, wrote the necessary passes and ordered the *Otter*'s tender to convey the widow on board the *Otter*, stationed at the Narrows. The widow, a few servants and their baggage were received aboard the *Otter* the next day.[1]

Captain Squires of the *Otter* sent the party ashore, escorted by British Marines under a flag of truce. The *Otter*'s party found Major James Hendrick, of the 6th Regiment of Continental Troops, stationed on the mainland near the Narrows. Hendrick respected the flag of truce and sent the widow, under escort of the 6th Virginia, to Williamsburg. By Wednesday evening, July 19, the widow Sprowl reached Williamsburg and went before Brigadier General Andrew Lewis. Lewis, a veteran commander who had served under Washington during the French and Indian Wars, cordially received Mrs. Sprowl. He listened to her request and then had his orderlies find the best accommodations possible in the overcrowded Virginia capital. Lewis expressed sympathy for the grieving widow. She had lost her husband, all her houses, possessions, and most of her servants; she no longer enjoyed the high social position to which she had been accustomed; she had been reduced to living aboard a rat-infested vessel for months; her eldest son was a prisoner of war; and now she was reduced to pleading through channels to visit her son. To Lewis, Catherine Sprowl was not a threat. She was not, however, simply a grieving widow. Lewis decided that the widow was a political matter not a military one. He sent his recommendations and other documentation to the "Committee of Safety." The Committee took the matter of widow Sprowl under advisement.[2]

While Sprowl's widow awaited consideration, four British seamen aboard the *Roebuck*'s tender, *Ranger*, stole a small boat and rowed up the Bay to the Maryland shore. The British deserters surrendered to the Maryland militia. All of the deserters were colonists, one from Boston and three from Philadelphia. They provided accurate information to the Maryland authorities on the numbers, armaments and forces in the floating town.[3]

On Friday, June 21, a large British vessel entered the Chesapeake bound for Dunmore. The troop transport *Oxford* headed for Hampton Roads, unaware of Dunmore's move to Gwynn's Island. On board the *Oxford* were 217 Scottish Highlanders with the 42nd Regiment—the Black Watch—and the 74th Regiment. Earlier the *Oxford*, part of General Clinton's southern expedition, was captured by the Continental Navy Brig *Andrea Doria* and a prize crew placed aboard. Later, the transport's crew, aided by the Highlanders, overwhelmed the prize crew. The *Oxford*'s crew and the Highlanders decided to join Dunmore's forces. On arrival in Hampton Roads, the *Oxford* learned of Dunmore's relocation, and they changed course to Gwynn's Island. Before they had sailed far, however, Virginia State Navy Captains James and Richard Barron in the *Patriot* and *Liberty* skillfully captured the *Oxford*. The Barrons sent the recaptured *Oxford* and the Highlanders up the James River to Williamsburg. The day the *Oxford* arrived at Williamsburg the "Committee of Safety" met and discussed several matters. These included the activities of loyalist John Goodrich and disposition of some of the *Oxford*'s supplies. News of the *Oxford*'s capture spread quickly and the atmosphere became festive. Under the guns of Continental forces, the uniformed Highlanders were marched as prisoners through Williamsburg. The town celebrated as if the Highlanders had been captured in battle. Their capture was, nonetheless a cheap and complete "victory" for the patriots.[4]

The "Committee of Safety" realized the *Oxford*'s capture was luck. A little better information by the British or less vigilance by the patriots would have provided Dunmore with 217 first rate troops with all their weapons and a large transport. That was precisely the type of reinforcement Dunmore and Hamond sought. As Highland troops, their arrival would have significantly improved the Scottish Earl's morale and prestige beyond their military value. As they discussed the *Oxford*, the Committee allowed Sprowl's widow to write her son, and they assured safe passage of the letter. However, the Committee of Safety expressly forbid her to travel to her son and ordered her return, as soon as possible, to the floating town. The Committee's decision sorely hurt and disappointed the grieving widow.[5]

A small schooner entered the Chesapeake just behind the *Oxford*. The schooner, with news from the *Liverpool*, sailed directly to Gwynn's Island and immediately reported to Hamond. The Commodore then sent word to the *Santa Barbara* for Eduardo and Gomalez to go aboard the *Roebuck* the following day. On Saturday, June 22, Eduardo of the *Santa Barbara* went aboard the *Roebuck* as requested. He experienced almost deferential treatment. He went to Hamond's cabin and, after polite formalities, the Commodore met privately with him. Hamond advised Eduardo of a further delay in the *Liverpool*'s arrival, and he suggested that the *Santa Barbara* proceed to Halifax, Nova Scotia. Eduardo knew Hamond's suggestion, if followed, would probably result in the loss of the *Santa Barbara*. Eduardo carefully controlled his emotions, but he staunchly refused to go, due to the poor condition of the vessel and the bad weather conditions likely to be encountered. Eduardo firmly believed that Hamond's suggestion was made "in the hope that we [*Santa Barbara*] would perish." Hamond was taken aback. He had not anticipated Eduardo's obstinacy, and he quickly demurred. Hamond politely dismissed Eduardo and told him that the matter would be taken up with Dunmore. Hamond requested Eduardo return for an answer within two days.[6]

On Sunday, Eduardo and Gomalez again dined aboard the *Dunmore*. In addition, the Governor's dinner guests included Hamond, his naval officers, Major Leslie of the 14th and other military officers, including those from the Queen's Own Loyal

Virginians and Dunmore's Royal Ethiopians. The Governor's stern cabin comfortably held the dozen or more guests and servants. Introductions began the evening followed by wines from the *Dunmore*'s considerable collection. The guests ate from Dunmore's fine china and used his sterling silver tableware. The occasion was the best the Royal Governor of Virginia could provide. Eduardo and Gomalez sat with some officers of the 14th who reflected on some of the events which had brought them to these circumstances. They told the Spaniards of the regiment's sacrifices, victories and losses at Norfolk, Kemp's Landing, Great Bridge, and other skirmishes. Eduardo was so comfortable that he "planned to throw caution to the wind . . ." and raise the question of their further detainment. He didn't get the chance. Suddenly, sails of two large vessels appeared, including a man-of-war, headed for the island. Hamond and his officers politely but quickly left the *Dunmore*. They were followed by the military officers and the Spaniards. The two ships proved to be British, the frigate *Lively* and the supply ship, *Levant*, and they brought news from New York to Hamond.[7]

Dunmore, his guests hastily departed, was reminded of the fragile nature of his naval and military support. He was Royal Governor of Virginia, but the King could, at any time, withdraw most of Dunmore's present sources of power and office. Indeed, Dunmore himself could be recalled. He still had his seat in Parliament and his estates in Scotland, but his request for reinstatement of regular military rank had been rejected years earlier. Scotland held few opportunities and Parliament had many members better connected, financed and with greater abilities than Dunmore. As Governor, Dunmore could assume rank, responsibility, prerogative and mission. Without the governorship, Dunmore's prospects lacked promise.

Encouraged by their recent conversations with the officers on the *Dunmore*, the Spaniards went ashore the following day. This was the Spaniards' first visit to the island and their initial observation of British efforts on Gwynn's Island. The British batteries, despite almost a month's activity, were not complete. The high number of sick and the poor conditions of those troops on duty shocked Eduardo. He claimed "dozens died daily." He observed "they (the British) would be forced to leave any day now."[8]

Across the Narrows, the patriots worked on their fortifications. The Spaniards watched as the *Otter* bombarded the patriot positions on the mainland. The naval guns did little damage to the earthworks. The high bank and the packed earth of the fort absorbed the *Otter*'s cannonballs. Few patriots, however, dared to work under such attack. The lack of return fire told the British that the patriots still lacked cannons large enough to threaten the fleet. Actually, the patriots did have large cannons, but mounting carriages had yet to be built.

While the Spaniards examined the island, Hamond studied the *Lively*'s dispatches and learned of Clinton's expedition to Charleston. The *Lively* was headed next to Charleston and Sir Peter Parker's fleet. Hamond began to formulate a plan of action. Hamond now had a current and complete summary of Clinton's strategy. Hamond wrote a brief note to Parker and told him that the return of the *Fowey* with Governor Eden would allow the *Roebuck*'s return to the Delaware and the relief of the *Orpheus* and *Liverpool*. The *Orpheus*, according to orders Hamond had just received, would soon return to Admiral Howe in New York. The *Liverpool* would be sent to Virginia to replace the *Roebuck*, get fresh provisions and replenish their crews from Dunmore's floating town.[9]

Hamond invited Captain Bishop of the *Lively* and Dunmore to dinner aboard the *Roebuck*. In addition to the official dispatches, the *Lively* brought the latest intelligence from Halifax and New York. Bishop and the dispatches provided the broad view of the American war. Hamond listened carefully to Bishop's news of the war. The *Lively* sailed early the next morning on Tuesday, June 25 for Charleston. Hamond then summoned the Spaniards to the *Roebuck*. Eduardo was characteristically apprehensive about the meeting. The decision discussed over two days before had been deferred by Hamond because "they were very occupied with the transport." Aboard the *Roebuck*, Hamond and Dunmore greeted Eduardo. Then Hamond guided Eduardo cordially by the arm to his private area of the *Roebuck*'s quarterdeck and said, "Dear Eduardo, good news." In a tone of confidentiality reminiscent of an earlier meeting, Hamond told Eduardo the necessary and relevant details of his plans. The *Liverpool*, which had originally seized the *Santa Barbara* and presumably still had the Spaniards 12,500 silver pesos aboard, would soon return to Gwynn's Island. "When she arrives, everything can be taken care of," said Hamond. A brief discussion on supplies ended when the *Roebuck*'s lookout sighted two vessels headed for the island. They brought news of the increased aggressiveness of the patriots. Hamond ordered the Spaniards returned to the *Santa Barbara*. Within a couple hours, the tender *Fincastle* and the British brig from Barbados, *William and Charles*, joined the fleet.[10]

The *William and Charles* had run hard aground on Willoughby's Point, later known as Willoughby Spit, about midnight, Sunday, June 23. The patriot militia under Major Andrew Leitch gathered twelve men, including naval Lieutenant Thomas Herbert, and commandeered a pilot boat. They boarded the stranded brig after dawn, assured themselves that the cargo was destined for Dunmore, and arrested the crew. On board, Leitch found "311 puncheons of rum, and a few barrels of limes." Leitch worked to lighten the brig in order to free it from Willoughby's Point. He sent four of the brig's crew ashore under guard. While Leitch and the militia worked on the brig, the British tender *Fincastle* spotted the activity and bore down swiftly to investigate. Lt. Wright quickly and correctly assessed the plight of the *William and Charles* and opened fire at the patriot vessel. The patriot pilot boat with some militia and two of the brig's crew aboard fled under fire from the *Fincastle*. On board the stranded brig, Lieutenant Herbert threw five puncheons overboard, hopefully to drift ashore, and got the remaining militia off in a ship's longboat, with the exception of one patriot who lingered too long in the hold.[11]

The *William and Charles* belonged to a Barbadian named Walsh and the crew were understandably elated when the *Fincastle* drove off the patriots, refloated the brig, and hoisted British colors. The patriots undoubtedly intended to seize the brig and confiscate a valuable cargo. The British recapture prevented a serious financial loss to the owners and crew. Crews and masters were paid for voyages completed, not attempted, and most owners could barely, if at all, survive the loss of one vessel with such a cargo.[12]

The return of the *Roebuck*'s tender and the arrival of the *Lively* and the *Levant* restored confidence to the British and loyalists. The sight of the *Fincastle* and the *William and Charles* under British colors bolstered morale at Gwynn's Island. Once the brig's cargo became known, morale rose further. The cargo of rum would quite adequately serve the needs of the fleet and the floating town. With water diminished in quantity and quality, the rum's arrival was timely. Hamond had earlier sent two long boats to gather water for his anticipated voyage to Delaware. In four days his working party had filled only six casks from the island, much of it poor in quality.[13]

That Tuesday evening militia Major Leitch reported the incident off Willoughby's Point to Colonel Hendricks, commander of the patriot forces in Hampton Roads. Hendricks promptly notified Brigadier General Lewis in Williamsburg. Hendricks also passed along his caustic observations on the Barbadian crew and their decided Tory sympathies.

Also on Tuesday evening, June 25, the *Ranger*, with two other tenders, returned from Maryland's Eastern Shore with almost 60 Maryland loyalists. Dunmore enlisted the loyalists into the Queen's Own Loyal Virginians. They received supplies from the *Levant* and erected tents near Fort Hamond. The patriots on the mainland saw the arrival of ships, supplies, and the many new tents in the camp as evidence of increased British strength, and they sent that message to General Lewis.[14]

The last several days' events renewed Dunmore's confidence, and he wrote his third letter to Lord George Germain. He summarized his actions between April 2 and Wednesday, June 26. Dunmore defended his relocation to Gwynn's Island and called the harbor incomparable. Like Hamond, he pointed out the sole weakness was "that it lies too near the Main (land)." He remarked that the fever had been "very Malignant and has carried off an incredible Number of People." Dunmore lamented the loss of the *Oxford* and her 217 Highlanders—". . . of what Service could they not have been to me here!" He also assured Germain that the Virginia Convention's recent unanimous resolution for independence did not reflect the majority of Virginians' views. The resolution would cause the "lower Class" to "willingly change sides." The show of support from Maryland's Eastern Shore was Dunmore's evidence. He cited his latest recruitment and his

Figure 8 The Lower Chesapeake Bay

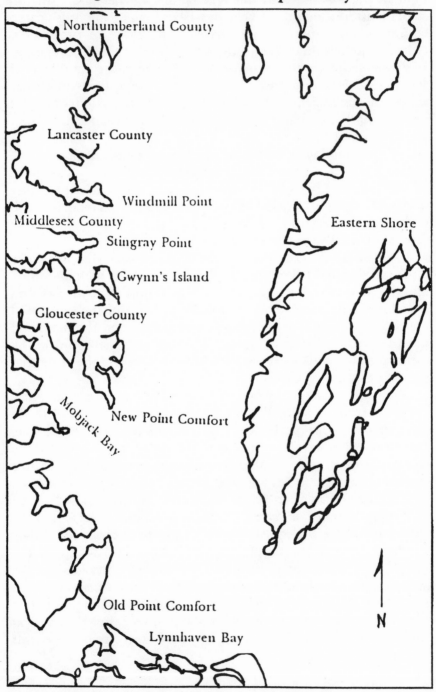

Figure 9 The Narrows

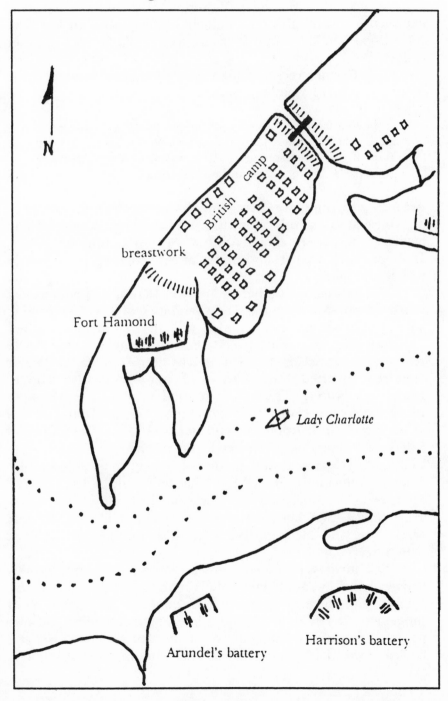

breastwork

British camp

Fort Hamond

Lady Charlotte

Arundel's battery

Harrison's battery

N

dispatch that morning of six vessels to "bring as many more as wish to serve his Majesty." Dunmore related to Germain the experiences of a number of prominent loyalists including the elder John Goodrich, Mr. Ralph Wormley and Philip Grymes, brother of John.[15]

John Grymes received high accolades from Dunmore. He described John Grymes as a person

> of the first family in this Country, of good fortune, but what is more valuable either, he is a most amiable Character, being a Man of the Strictest honor, of an excellent disposition and good parts, Brave, Active and enterprizing.

According to Dunmore "Mr. John Grymes is the only person of any consequence in this colony that has joined me." Dunmore had evidently forgotten about Andrew Sprowl's support. Worse, Dunmore took a harsh and unexplained action against Sprowl's widow and family.[16]

Only days before, Catherine Sprowl had returned under a flag of truce from Williamsburg. The Committee of Safety's refusal to allow her to see her son, coupled with the recent death of her husband, severely upset her. The best she could do now was to return to her vessel and be comforted by friends and family. Major Hendrick escorted the widow and her servants to one of Dunmore's officers. The officer refused to allow the widow to rejoin the floating town. He advised the widow that Dunmore had given specific instructions to send her back to the Committee of Safety in Williamsburg. Shocked, the widow sent a message to Commodore Hamond and requested him to intercede for her. Hamond reluctantly advised her "that he has no right to do so." Spurned by the Americans and now exiled by Dunmore the widow grew angry. She obtained a notary from the fleet, Thomas McCullock, and filed a petition "against the Conduct of Lord Dunmore."[17]

On Thursday, June 27, aboard the *Roebuck*, Catherine Sprowl, widow of Andrew, availed herself of the right of a free born British subject and formally recorded Dunmore's incredibly poor judgement. In addition to denying her return to the fleet, she also accused Dunmore of failing to execute her late husband's will and codicil. Two of Hamond's lieutenants witnessed the document.

Hamond helped to calm the widow and assisted her in preparing realistic plans in the face of Dunmore's inexplicable intransigence. Her return to Williamsburg was valueless so Hamond had the widow placed aboard the schooner *Betsey*, soon to sail to Glasgow.

The following day, the widow wrote Hamond from the schooner *Betsey*. Her personal correspondence used even harsher language than the petition. She claimed Dunmore "barbarously condemned" her to leave the floating town though he (Dunmore) "was himself but a little (while) ago protected and supported (by) my ever Dear deceased Husband." She repeatedly accused Dunmore of denying her basic rights to trial or hearing as an English subject. She claimed the Governor would not even allow "her to take a family inventory or to pack up my own parafamalia (sic)!" Prior to his death, Andrew Sprowl cautioned his wife to leave the fleet "but not till she had settled his affairs so as not to be lost to her or his [Andrew's] heirs . . ." Sprowl's estate was still considerable, despite the loss and condemnation of his property in Virginia. After he received the widow's letter, Hamond spoke again to Dunmore but "he could not bring him to reason." Hamond "therefore advised her to go directly home and apply for Justice, and that he (Hamond) would answer (be a witness) when called upon."[18]

The focus of the dispute was probably the rivalry between two powerful individuals for respect and authority from the floating town's constituency. Sprowl had served and directed the largest association of Virginia merchants for decades. He had also served numerous official and prestigious offices under at least five royal governors. He ran the largest naval and maritime shipyard in the colonies. His political position, wealth and longevity had bestowed great social prominence on the Sprowls. In the floating town, many loyalists regarded Sprowl unofficially as the "Lord Lieutenant" of Gosport and the "Lieutenant-Governor" of Virginia. Surrounded by business associates, friends and family, Andrew Sprowl still commanded great respect. Lord Dunmore was a proud and arrogant man. Appointed by the King as Royal Governor, he commanded the colonists. However, the circumstances of life in the floating town wore away at the relationship between the new governor and the old prince of the merchant community. The widow Sprowl wrote to Hamond of her husband's sacrifice and death, ". . . may not that satisfy a jealous Governor without persecuting his poor widow . . ." Naturally, Dunmore prevailed.[19]

Allies and Adversaries

Early on Saturday morning, June 29th, a large sail was sighted to the north and so reported to Hamond, who was still asleep. The *Roebuck*, accompanied by the transport ship *William*, got underway toward the sail. At 7 a.m., the *Roebuck* ran aground on the Windmill Point sandbar. Hamond ordered all ships' boats out to tow her off the bar. The tide ebbed and the *Roebuck* settled further. By noon, she was hard aground. As the large sail approached the stranded *Roebuck*, Hamond recognized the returning *Fowey*. The *Roebuck* and *Fowey* exchanged signals and Captain Montague of the *Fowey* sent several ship's boats to help free the *Roebuck*. Just after high tide at 6 p.m., the boat crews from the *Fowey* and *Roebuck* pulled the *Roebuck* off the bar. The *Roebuck* anchored in the Rappahannock and Hamond inspected the damage. The *Roebuck* was seaworthy. The *William* and *Fowey* anchored nearby. That evening Captain Montague and his "Excellency Governor Eden" met with Hamond aboard the *Roebuck*. Captain Montague described his activities connected with Eden's removal from Annapolis.[1]

Light winds had slowed the *Fowey*'s passage from Gwynn's Island to Maryland. On Saturday, June 22, she sailed from the Patuxant River and reached Annapolis at 8 p.m. The *Fowey* anchored near Thomas Point. Reports of the arrival of a large British warship quickly reached Governor Eden. At dawn the next morning, Montague hoisted a flag of truce to the peak of the *Fowey*'s foremast and then sent the longboat with a lieutenant, also under a flag of truce, to the Governor. The lieutenant carried a letter which outlined Montague's authority and instructions from Hamond. At 11 a.m., the longboat returned to the *Fowey*. At 4 p.m. the longboat again was sent ashore to await the Governor. Soon many members of the Maryland Council, Assembly and other citizens accompanied Governor Eden to the harbor. Eden later recalled their parting as most affectionate and peaceful. At 6 p.m., the Governor of Maryland, Robert Eden, boarded HMS *Fowey* to a thirteen-gun salute. The Governor expected his baggage, personal possessions and servants to follow the next day. In his absence, Governor Eden placed his secretary, Robert Smith, in charge of the colony's affairs.[2]

During the night, Eden's plans went awry. Five indentured servants and a militia deserter stole a boat, rowed to the *Fowey* and were received on board. The next morning, several petitions from the shore reached Captain Montague which requested return of the runaways. Montague was in a difficult position. He had received the Maryland Governor but not the Governor's baggage and servants. Hamond had ordered Montague to take "his (Eden's) servants on board as well as any other affected subjects to His Majesty that may claim your protection." Hamond's instructions clearly covered the runaways. Both Eden and Montague responded to the petitions. They would return the boat but not the subjects. Montague restated his desire to simply get the Governor's personal effects and servants. Then the *Fowey* would depart.[3]

The Maryland Convention, which met less than a mile from the *Fowey*, read the petitions and responses that same Monday afternoon. They acted quickly and decisively. The Convention concluded that the British had violated the truce. They ordered the Maryland warship *Defence* on alert and established a patrol in Annapolis and nearby waters to prevent raids from the *Fowey*'s boats. A militia company was sent south to alert all inhabitants of the *Fowey*'s truce violation and to guard property from seizure. All correspondence between Eden, Montague and others would be published. The Convention prohibited communication with the *Fowey*, and worse for Montague and Eden, allowed no "baggage or effects belonging to Robert Eden, Esq. . . . to be carried on board" the *Fowey*. Montague and the Maryland Convention had reached an impasse. Each took specific, firm positions which only compromise or negotiation could alter.

Montague was unaware of the rapid escalation of the runaway incident. Tuesday morning he had the *Fowey*'s sails dried, surveyed some supplies and sent a small working party ashore to fill ten empty hogsheads with water. The Maryland militia promptly seized the empty hogsheads but allowed the working party to return to the *Fowey*. When the seizure was reported to Montague, he wrote a terse letter to the President of the Maryland Council of Safety, Daniel of St. Thomas Jennifer. Montague accused Maryland of breaking the truce and expressed his "great astonishment" that the Governor's baggage "is still alongside the wharf." He requested an immediate answer. No answer was forthcoming. The Convention had forbidden communications with the *Fowey*. While he waited, Montague read and reread his instructions from Hamond. In the event of an insult, Montague had discretion to "act against them as you may think proper." Still no communication came back from the Council of Safety.[4]

That night two additional runaways also stole a boat and sought asylum aboard the *Fowey*. Peter Crawford and James McCaskie seized a boat and forced its owner to take them to the *Fowey*. After they reached the *Fowey*, the boat and owner were immediately released. The runaways informed the British of rumored action against the *Fowey*. Rumors of the State's call to readiness and the dispatch of the *Defence* caused Montague to seek the Bay's open waters immediately. On Wednesday morning Montague sent a deposition of Crawford's and McCaskie's action to the Convention and hoisted anchor. The *Fowey* called briefly at the port of Oxford on Maryland's Eastern Shore. There, four enterprising Marylanders went aboard the *Fowey* and offered sheep and hogs for sale as well as gifts to the Crown and the Governor. A deal was struck. The Marylanders gathered the stock and delivered them to the *Fowey*. Between the deal and the delivery, the local Committee of Safety received word of the Convention's embargo of all trade and communication with the *Fowey*. Maryland militia Captain James Kindman set out with twenty men to stop the deal but met the loyalist party as they returned from the *Fowey*. Confronted by the armed committee, the party acted contritely and placed themselves in the custody of the Convention to answer for the incident. On July 2, the four appeared before the Convention and were acquitted of wrongdoing. The *Fowey*'s larder, however, was richer by 22 live animals. The *Fowey* returned to the open Bay in light to moderate winds. She sailed south and spotted the *Roebuck* on Saturday, June 29.[5]

Hamond was pleased at the relative success in extracting Eden. Montague returned with the Governor, eight loyalists, fresh meat, and no damage or losses, except for the empty water casks. The *Fowey* had received provocation but had offered none. On Sunday morning, the *Roebuck, Fowey,* and *William,* returned to Gwynn's Island. By now most of the supply ship *Levant*'s supplies had been used or distributed. The *Fowey* depleted the remainder. The *Levant* was a comfortable ship, and it eventually became Eden's residence. Eden took no active role at Gwynn's Island and seldom spoke to either Hamond or Dunmore while he remained in the floating town. The loss of his baggage forced Eden to seek personal articles as well as clothing from the fleet. Hamond, Montague and fellow officers eased Eden's needs to avoid his further embarrassment. Most important, the *Fowey*'s return now provided Hamond with his opportunity to cruise to the Delaware.[6]

The zeal of the Eastern Shore loyalists and their increasing numbers pleased both Dunmore and Hamond. Reports of similar loyalist strength came from Delaware. For weeks Hamond had counseled the Eastern Shore loyalists not to defy the patriots and he had withheld direct support from them. With the *Fowey* back, Eden secure, and the recent string of fortuitous events, Hamond decided to further delay his return to the Delaware. He ordered Montague, his tender *Fincastle* and several other tenders to bolster the Eastern Shore loyalists and distribute weapons among them. By July 2, Montague had gathered his fleet and was underway for a rendezvous in Tangier Sound. Hamond also knew Montague needed a chance at action. His recent foray to Annapolis was a credit to Montague's ability as a commander. On the Eastern Shore Montague could exercise his crew almost without restrictions. Montague needed an opportunity to work as a fleet commander. When Hamond returned to the Delaware, Montague would be commodore and the experience of independent

Figure 10 The Upper Chesapeake Bay

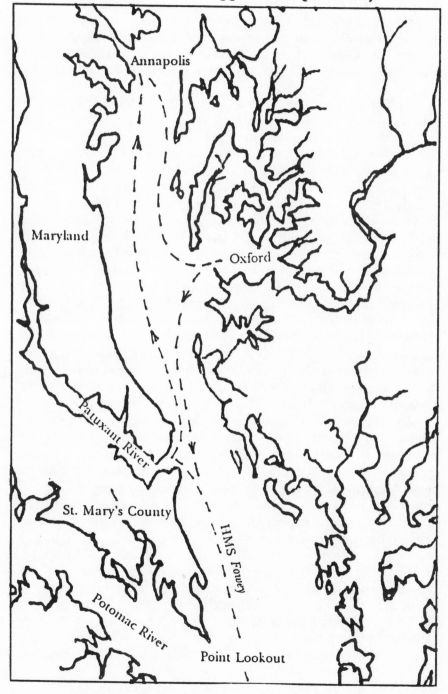

command on the Eastern Shore would serve him well. Hamond
decided to sail for the Delaware once Montague had returned.[7]

As Montague sailed, the Virginia Council of Safety ordered
the two eighteen-pound cannons at Gwynn's Island to the Potomac
for use by Colonel George Mason. Those two cannons, still
unmounted on the American mainland, were the only weapons
capable of inflicting damage on all ships in the floating town. The
patriot battery, near the Narrows, commanded Milford Haven. It
held 5 six- and nine-pound cannon. These were capable of hitting
Fort Hamond as well as the two small batteries on the Haven. The
fleet lay beyond Fort Hamond, within range of the larger cannon.
The six- and nine-pounders might reach some ships, but they
would inflict little damage. The eighteen-pounders could strike
and damage most ships in the anchorage as far as Cherry Point.
The removal of the large cannon would allow the British to move
unhindered across much of the island and anchorage. Without
large cannon, only an American assault across the Haven in force,
supported by numerous naval vessels, would have a chance for
success. State navy vessels under construction in Virginia and
Maryland might successfully challenge the *Otter* and the smaller
vessels, but only the Continental Navy had vessels capable of
challenging the *Fowey*. However, no American vessel could hope to
successfully challenge the *Roebuck*. The British defense needed the
Roebuck and the American offense needed the large cannon. Both
intended to soon leave the Gwynn's Island area, but neither side
knew of the other's plan.[8]

In early July, the Governor sent a letter to General Lewis in
Williamsburg under a flag of truce. Dunmore offered a prisoner
exchange. He wanted the Highlanders recently captured in the
Oxford but knew his patriot prisoners were too few in number.
Dunmore arrogantly suggested that if he was given credit for the
deficit in prisoners he would turn over prisoners, when captured,
to the extent of the credit. On Friday, July 5th, Lewis's response
reached Gwynn's Island. Lewis rejected the prisoner exchange and
countered with a demand that Dunmore withdraw from the island.
At the same time the Americans revealed the battery which
commanded Milford Haven. One cannon projected from each of
the battery's five casements. A hundred yards west of this battery,
on higher wooded ground, the battery of eighteen-pounders
remained hidden but still incomplete.[9]

By early July, almost 2,000 Virginia militia and Continental troops watched Gwynn's Island. Responsibility for Virginia and the South belonged to Major General Charles Lee. Under him, Brigadier General Andrew Lewis commanded Virginia's forces and Colonel Daingerfield held immediate responsibility for the forces around Gwynn's Island. Several possibilities concerned the Americans. It appeared to the Americans that the British forces at Gwynn's Island increased daily. Vessels arrived and departed daily, and the number of tents in the camp near Fort Hamond grew. British troops could cross the Narrows and attack the mainland, or board the fleet and land somewhere else on the Bay. So far, the influx of recruits to the island had been gradual, but a transport or two, such as the *Oxford*, could considerably affect the local balance of military power. The patriot troops around Gwynn's Island were positioned defensively. Lewis was unwilling to commit all his available forces to the Gloucester region because of British mobility and the imminent possibility of significant reinforcements.[10]

The British southern expedition, assembled in the winter of 1775, had arrived in North Carolina in May 1776. Lieutenant General Henry Clinton commanded the expedition. During June, General Clinton's activity off Charleston, South Carolina, left little doubt that invasion there was imminent. General Lee traveled from Williamsburg to Charleston and spent much of June preparing Charleston's defense. The British attack finally came on June 28. By midnight the same day, the British prematurely acknowledged failure but lingered in the area for another three weeks. For the patriots, the next destination of the British forces and the possibility of a renewed attack on Charleston, still existed in early July. News of the patriot victory in Charleston did not reach Williamsburg until after July 9th.[11]

To the north, the colonists watched events in Philadelphia. At the Continental Congress, Virginia took the lead in urging independence. Thomas Jefferson worked throughout June on drafts of various documents for use by the Congress. On June 7, Virginia's Richard Henry Lee moved for a resolution of independence. On July 2, 1776, the Congress adopted Lee's resolution, and on July 4, it accepted Thomas Jefferson's draft of the Declaration of Independence. Official news of the Declaration reached Williamsburg by July 19, but unofficial information traveled much faster. Most colonists in late June and early July were aware of the movement of the colonies toward independence.

The only question was when it would occur.[12]

In Williamsburg, the Virginia Convention had unanimously adopted a resolution for independence on May 15, 1776. This became the mandate for Virginia's delegates to the Continental Congress. Virginia, now independent, began work on a new state government. In June, the Convention passed George Mason's Declaration of Rights. This document influenced constitutional provisions in other states as well as later in the American Bill of Rights. The later French Rights of Man and the Citizen owed much to George Mason, and in the twentieth century, the United Nations adapted portions of Mason's work in its Statement on Human Rights. Virginia's political leadership was extremely busy and fragmented in June 1776. Washington commanded the Continental Army outside New York while much of Virginia's remaining leadership was divided between the Virginia Convention in Williamsburg and the Continental Congress in Philadelphia.[13]

On June 29, the Convention adopted a constitution for the new Commonwealth of Virginia. The same day it chose Patrick Henry as the new Commonwealth's Governor. In late June and early July, the Virginia forces surrounding Gwynn's Island had much to discuss as they watched the British. The steps taken by the Convention and the Continental Congress were, literally, revolutionary. The Colony of Virginia and over 150 years of British rule disappeared in early July 1776. Independence further polarized undecided Virginians. Independence also encouraged military action against the British. The Continental Congress prepared orders to send military units from Williamsburg and around Gwynn's Island north to join Washington's army at New York. If the large cannon and Continental regiments withdrew, some patriots feared Dunmore might go on the offense in Gloucester. On July 6, however, Richard Henry Lee hinted of imminent action against Dunmore. He wrote to Samuel Adams, "Our Devil Dunmore is as he was, but we expect readily to make him move his quarters."[14]

On Sunday afternoon, July 7, the *Fowey, Fincastle,* and other tenders returned from the Eastern Shore. Montague's expedition had been successful. He brought approximately 100 volunteers, many cattle and fresh supplies. Two of the loyalist leaders told Hamond they could raise more recruits. They sought commissions from Dunmore as captains in order to get credit for their recruiting efforts. News of the arrival of further fresh loyalists and supplies on Gwynn's Island traveled quickly to General Lewis in Williamsburg.[15]

Lewis still hesitated to reinforce his Gloucester forces. Lewis worried that Clinton would unexpectedly arrive to reinforce Dunmore or attack elsewhere. Earlier in the spring, Clinton had visited Dunmore to ascertain the military preparedness of the Southern Governors. Clinton originally intended to support Dunmore in an attack in Virginia, but he was persuaded by Sir Peter Parker to attack Charleston instead. Lewis knew of earlier intercepted correspondence which reflected Clinton's ideas. Lewis was unaware of the British failure at Charleston.

However, as a result of the renewed British activity over the past two weeks, the continuing supplies of men, vessels, and food to the island, and the renewed presence of powerful British warships, General Andrew Lewis took the offensive. With the news of the latest arrivals at Gwynn's Island, Lewis left Williamsburg late Monday afternoon. He arrived at dusk at the patriot fortifications opposite the Narrows. He ordered the troops to complete the battery of eighteen-pounders. They worked through the night. Lewis met with battery commanders and regimental officers and ordered preparations for an attack on the island the next morning. Militia Colonel McClanahan raised the problem of troop transport to the island. The Americans had few vessels capable of carrying troops from the mainland to the island. The *Lady Charlotte* and two other armed tenders still patrolled the Haven. The patriots had nothing available locally to challenge any of those British vessels. Lewis ordered Major Harrison to move two field cannon to a point opposite the east entrance of Milford Haven. Lewis intended to bottle up the three British patrol vessels and destroy them with his six- and nine-pound cannon. The eighteen-pounders would hold the Royal Navy vessels off and neutralize Fort Hamond. Lewis also ordered a search of surrounding waters to locate boats for troop transport. Lewis planned to send boats with patriot troops across the Haven, drive the British forces to their beachhead, and capture those who failed to reach their vessels.[16]

Hamond also worked hard on the 8th and into the early hours of the 9th. With the *Fowey*'s return, he made last-minute preparations to leave Gwynn's Island. He had finally obtained sufficient water for the *Roebuck* and he had asked Dunmore for permission to withdraw the *Roebuck*'s marines who guarded the beach. Dunmore agreed, and the marines reboarded the *Roebuck* Monday afternoon. Hamond also suggested in his letter to Dunmore that the sooner the *Roebuck* got to the Delaware, the sooner the *Liverpool* would be at Gwynn's Island. Hamond by now was aware that the *Liverpool* had sailed to New York to refit and recruit. Both the Spaniards and Dunmore still thought the *Liverpool* would replace the *Roebuck*. Hamond also kept an eye on the weather. The weather remained very warm with light airs, but a change was anticipated. High tide would be at about noon on Tuesday, July 9. That would be the best time to get the *Roebuck* underway with her tender and whatever other vessels wished to accompany her.[17]

Andrew Lewis also thought about the next day. He had a sense of history and timing. Twenty-one years earlier, on July 9, British General Edward Braddock had been attacked and soundly defeated by a smaller force of French and Indians. Lewis, along with George Washington, had served in that campaign. The anniversary of the defeat of Braddock was a good day to begin an attack on the British at Gwynn's Island. All that was needed was a target of opportunity. That too, presented itself.[18]

The *Otter* badly needed her hull cleaned. Below the waterline marine growth reduced her speed and weakened the hull. She needed to be "careened," and the sandy shallows of the island presented an ideal opportunity. Her guns and equipment were removed, and she was beached in the island's shallows as cleaning parties worked on her. Some of the *Otter*'s guns were mounted on the *Dunmore*, and the Governor's ship now stood guard near the Narrows. In the still, warm summer air, the *Dunmore*'s stern was directly opposite the hidden American battery. The ship's name, in four-inch-high letters, was plainly visible from the battery only several hundred yards distant. The Governor sat in the large stern cabin. With good eyesight, the patriots in the battery at the Narrows could see Dunmore through the stern windows.[19]

7

Patriot Offensive

At dawn on Tuesday, July 9th, the tide was low and no breeze stirred. The temperature was already above 80° and the air humid. Although unsure what consequences might ensue, General Andrew Lewis personally aimed and then fired the first cannon directly at the *Dunmore*. The eighteen-pound iron cannonball smashed through the weakest part of any sailing vessel, her stern, and traveled almost the length of the vessel. The second cannonball also hit the *Dunmore* in the stern. Dunmore came very close to death. One cannonball killed his sailing master instantly. The first two cannonballs ripped a huge hole in Dunmore's cabin and splinters sprayed everywhere. The cannonball and splinters destroyed Dunmore's fine china and slightly wounded the governor. At the same time, the other American battery opened fire on the camp, Fort Hamond, the fleet, and the *Dunmore*. The cannonballs flew across the fort and mowed down tents. In the camp the inexperienced troops and newly recruited loyalists became panicked and confused. No one had anticipated the American attack.[1]

At the first shot, Hamond ordered the *Roebuck*'s boats away to tow vessels out of range. His first concern was the *Otter*, careened on Gwynn's Island and extremely vulnerable to attack. There was also the *Dunmore* to think about. The American batteries fired every few minutes. Each cannon had to be cleaned, loaded, primed, repositioned, aimed and fired. The larger cannon took even longer. Remarkably, the *Dunmore* quickly returned the fire from her deck cannon. But her cannon were too small, the crew "too weak and raw" to be accurate, and the patriots' fortifications too well situated for much damage to occur. Dunmore cut both his anchor cables and ordered his boats to tow the ship out of cannon range. Meanwhile, nearly every shot from the American batteries struck the *Dunmore*. In the half-hour it took to tow her out of range, over a dozen cannonballs hulled the *Dunmore*, all nine- and eighteen-pounders. Some caused serious damage. Aboard the *Dunmore* at least one person died, three were seriously wounded, and several others were slightly wounded including Dunmore himself. The total casualties did not overwhelm the crew of twenty-five but the suddenness and shock of the attack was devastating.[2]

Captain Dohickey Arundel, a Frenchman, commanded the Narrows battery. Acting Captain Charles Harrison commanded the Haven battery. As the *Dunmore* crept out of range, Harrison next targeted the *Otter* and then other ships in the floating town. The *Otter* was hit several times but with her cannon removed, was quickly towed by the *Roebuck*'s boats away from the island. It would take a full day to restore her to battle readiness. The patriots' heavy cannon also hit the large loyalist ship *Logan*. Often cannonballs passed completely through merchant vessels' hulls. Later several of the merchantmen were destroyed due to the damage. The fleet was in a panic. Low tide and no wind severely restricted the ability to maneuver the vessels. The only effective way to move the vessels was towing. Few loyalists wanted to leave their vessels or the shore to row a small boat amidst cannon fire. Even shots which missed the target usually struck another vessel in the crowded anchorage. The *Fowey* and *Roebuck* remained out of range. The largest cannon in the fleet were the *Roebuck*'s eighteen-pounders. Against the patriot shore batteries, with their higher elevation, in confined waters, with no wind, the Royal Navy ships had little chance to effectively return the American batteries' fire.[3]

Arundel's battery soon came under fire from Fort Hamond. Arundel fired three successive nine-pound cannonballs into the fort and silenced it. The British troops there withdrew to the large adjacent breastwork still under construction. Next, Arundel turned his fire on the British in battery 1, which soon also stopped firing. Arundel retrained his guns on the camp and continued a steady fire on the loyalists and regulars. His battery was joined by Harrison's. Together, their fire crisscrossed the camp and did much damage. Amazingly, no British were killed. After over an hour and a half, the patriot batteries ceased firing. They had fired almost two hundred rounds.[4]

The effect of their attack surprised Lewis and the Americans. Organized British resistance crumbled. The British abandoned their camp and crowded onto the beaches while they waited to board vessels. Only the British guard vessels in Milford Haven and an absence of troop transports prevented a landing by the Americans. Lewis met with the regimental leaders to find more suitable troop transports. The patriot batteries resumed fire two hours later, but there were few targets.

During this cannonade, Captain Arundel fired an experimental weapon of his own design. Arundel made a mortar from several pieces of dense hardwood banded together with wide iron rings. Then he lined the wooden mortar's barrel with an iron sleeve. He knew it wouldn't be as durable as a solid cast-iron mortar, but he hoped it might last for several rounds. The iron bands and sleeves could be reused or easily recast, and there was plenty of wood for new mortars. Arundel's mortars could be made quickly, without the necessary iron foundry and specialized workers, and they could be easily transported due to their comparatively light weight. Several officers, including General Lewis, doubted the weapon's safety. They tried to discourage Arundel from firing his weapon. Undaunted, the Frenchman personally loaded and then fired the mortar. The mortar exploded and Captain Arundel died instantly. Arundel's death temporarily halted any further patriot firing at the island. Lieutenant Samuel Denny assumed command of Arundel's battery.[5]

With the British in obvious retreat General Lewis redoubled efforts to locate troop transports. He ordered all available boats and canoes brought to nearby Stutts and Lane's Creeks. During the night all the improvised transports were gathered at Lower Windmill Point. The mobile battery sent there earlier would provide covering fire for any troop movement over the water. Two six-pounders were set up near one of Lower Windmill Point's four windmills. During the evening, several companies of the 7th Virginia Regiment gathered near the two field pieces. These preparations sealed the fate of the British patrol vessels on the Haven.[6]

When the early morning's firing ceased, Hamond gathered Dunmore, Eden and the military officers, Leslie and Byrd, on board the *Roebuck*. In the hot, humid cabin, they quickly devised a plan of action. The group agreed that the island "was no longer tenable" and should be immediately evacuated. Hamond proposed to proceed to New York with the naval and transport vessels while all others would be convoyed to St. Augustine or some other safe place. Dunmore initially objected, but Eden supported Hamond and the plan passed with no further debate. Many of the vessels were unseaworthy, most without water, the general conditions reminiscent of the evacuation from Hampton Roads only seven weeks earlier. All present at the meeting agreed it was impossible to reach a state of readiness while under fire in a crowded anchorage. Hamond suggested St. George's Island in the Potomac as a staging area for the voyage from the Chesapeake. It was less than a day's sail to St. George's. Hamond recommended that the group assembled begin preparations to leave the next day. Except for his lone objection at this critical meeting, Dunmore's participation was minimal. Nominally, he should have led and guided the course of action. In many similar situations, Dunmore had dominated the circumstances and behaved autocratically. The experience of cannonballs smashing through his quarters, the death of his boatswain, and his wounds as well as other wounded on his ship had shaken his confidence. When he objected to separation of the military and non-military vessels, his colleague, Governor Eden, whom Dunmore had rescued, sided against him. He stood alone and was disregarded. The decision to leave Gwynn's Island and eventually the Bay signalled the end of Dunmore's tenure as Virginia's Royal Governor.[7]

Major Leslie of the 14th and Major Byrd of Dunmore's Royal Ethiopians waited until dark to retrieve as much from the camp as possible. Leslie posted a guard at Fort Hamond to discourage raids from the mainland and to prevent looting. All useful materials were collected, cannon brought from the batteries and remaining troops embarked on the transports. Hamond, Montague and the naval officers got the vessels ready to sail and identified those unseaworthy due to damage by the cannon fire or other conditions. The loyalists scurried about and gathered what they could from the island. Dunmore spent much time repairing the damage to his vessel. When dawn came, the British had not completed the evacuation of all men and material.[8]

Just after dawn on Wednesday, July 10, Acting Captain Harrison opened fire on the three vessels in the Haven from his two field pieces on Lower Windmill Point. The schooner, though armed, ran into Barn Creek and the crew abandoned and set fire to her. The sloop *Lady Charlotte*, well-armed and with a naval crew, exchanged fire with Harrison's battery. The tide was low and the sloop went aground on a sandbar in range of the battery. General Lewis acted on the opportunity and sent orders to troops of the 7th Virginia nearby. Captain Gregory Smith's Company, 7th Virginia, manned a half-dozen log canoes and began the assault. The *Lady Charlotte*'s crew saw the canoes headed toward them and quickly left in their longboat for the island. The canoes moved very swiftly over the calm waters and soon overtook the longboat. After some small arms exchange, most of the sloop's crew escaped ashore in the shallow waters but several were captured by Smith's troops. Those captured included some wounded and the nephew of Captain Squire of the *Otter*.[9]

On shore, the loyalists at the Hill's Creek battery, its two cannon removed, helplessly watched the capture of the *Lady Charlotte*. They also mistakenly thought Smith's forces were the first wave of an invasion. The British took to their heels shouting "The damned shirtmen are coming." Several of Smith's canoes cut off the last remaining British vessel in the Haven. The small pilot boat and her crew offered no resistance. Some canoes brought back the sloop's longboat and prisoners while others towed the *Lady Charlotte* off the sandbank.[10]

With the naval forces eliminated, Lewis ordered an assault on the island. Lieutenant Colonel Alexander McClanahan took a battalion of the 7th Virginia and manned all the remaining canoes brought from Stutts and Lane's Creeks. Less than three dozen vessels, mostly canoes, were available. Almost 250 American troops got ashore on the island before noon. As the Americans marched from the east end of the island to the west, the remaining British forces on the island boarded the fleet. Major Byrd, commanding

Figure 11 The Bombardment, July 9

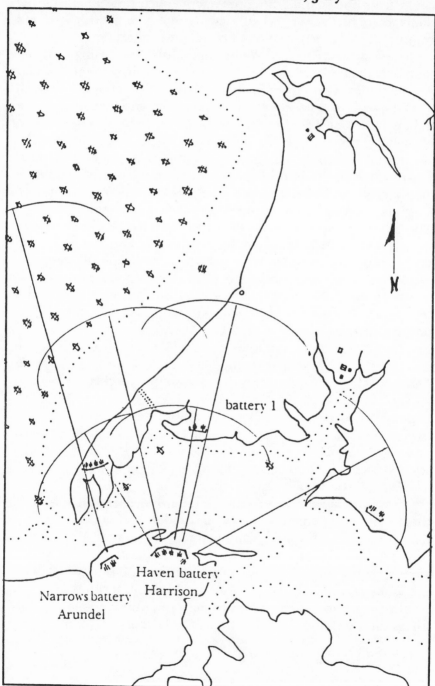

battery 1

Haven battery
Harrison

Narrows battery
Arundel

Figure 12 The Assault, July 10

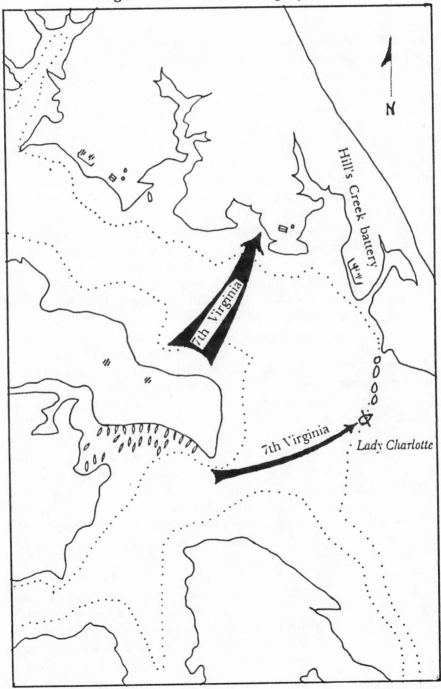

Dunmore's Royal Ethiopians reportedly led his unit's retreat from a cart, due to illness. British troops manned Fort Hamond and the unfinished breastwork adjacent until the island was nearly evacuated. As the patriots approached the fort from the Haven, the remaining British retreated. They rowed to the fleet as the Americans reached the beach.[11]

On landing, McClanahan's troops "were struck with horrour (sic) at the number of dead bodies, in a state of putrefaction (sic), strewed all the way from their battery to Cherry Point." While at Gwynn's Island, smallpox and jail fever had continued to ravage the floating town. The summer heat, lack of good water, inadequate medical supplies, and absence of treatment skills increased the suffering. Men, women, and some infants were found dead or dying. Many dead had not been buried, while others had been buried in mass graves which held several persons. One American counted over 130 such graves. Many never got a burial and were simply dumped overboard from the fleet.[12]

Others, diseased and crazed with thirst, had crawled to the shore and drank sea water—a certain, slow death. The Americans found a woman with a nursing infant, both dying. One American reported "such a scene of misery, distress, and cruelty my eyes never beheld . . ." The smell and fear of contamination caused the patriots to set fire to the brush hovels in the quarantine camp. Unfortunately, some of the hovels still contained dying but not dead victims. About mid-point on the north shore, a large grave, carefully tended, marked the remains of Andrew Sprowl, the late "Lord of Gosport."[13]

The British left much behind. The Americans recovered a nine-pound cannon, several tents including some marquees or large officer's tents, much baggage and numerous small arms. They also found abandoned storehouses, bakeries, a hospital structure, and a windmill under construction. Loyalist John Grymes abandoned almost three dozen "servants," horses, cattle, furniture and personal possessions. With all troops aboard, Hamond signalled the fleet to rendezvous with the *Roebuck* and *Fowey* south of Stingray Point. For the rest of the afternoon, just over one hundred vessels attempted to comply. Hamond, perhaps softened by Governor Eden's support of his earlier proposal to quit the island, ordered Captain Thomas of the *Levant* to obey any request of Eden's for his passage home.[14]

As the fleet got underway, Continental Army Lt. Denny saw an opportunity. He took command of the *Lady Charlotte* and, with some men from his battery and other volunteers, sailed into Hill's Bay to challenge the British fleet. He hoisted the American flag over the British colors on the *Lady Charlotte*. The British were chagrined to see their sloop now under American colors, yet no Royal Navy vessel could reply to the challenge because of the fleet's immediate needs. Lt. Denny was also careful to remain within range of the patriot eighteen-pounders at the "Narrows." Only the *Otter* lay between the recovering fleet and the island. Just after 4 p.m., the *Lady Charlotte*, well out of range of the *Otter*'s guns, fired her broadside at the *Otter*. It did no physical damage. Captain Squires recognized the sloop on which his nephew had served. Not knowing his nephew's fate, Squires fired a single gun in reply to the sloop's challenge. The presence of the aggressive *Lady Charlotte* and American occupation of the island confirmed Hamond's decision to relocate. British crews worked through the night to make as many vessels as possible seaworthy. Hamond ordered those not found seaworthy burned. The patriots later salvaged some of these vessels, hastily abandoned but not destroyed, and recovered some items of value from them.[15]

The following morning, July 11, the *Roebuck* signalled the fleet to get underway. The *Fowey* repeated the signal to the *Otter* and two hours later, at 10 a.m., the fleet hoisted anchor. As the fleet got underway, an important vessel, full of flour, ran aground. Hamond sent the *Otter* to assist her. The *Otter*'s crew spent the entire day working unsuccessfully to free the vessel. In order to lighten the vessel, they heaved over part of the precious cargo. As the *Otter*'s crew worked aboard the flour ship, they saw smoke rising from the island. The smoke came from the diseased encampment which the Americans burned to purge the island of the British infection.[16]

The rest of the fleet, reduced to 96 vessels according to the Spaniard, Eduardo, sailed northward. As the day progressed, the winds grew stronger. At 4 p.m., the *Dunmore*'s mizzen mast, damaged earlier by the cannon fire, gave way. The main topmast followed and the *Dunmore* fell behind the fleet. Hamond sent a lieutenant and several skilled seamen to assist the Governor and bring the *Dunmore* back under control. At 8 p.m., just below Point Lookout, Hamond signalled the fleet to anchor. The wind and seas had reached gale strength and many vessels had only one anchor. In the hasty departure from Gwynn's Island, many vessels had cut their anchor cables so as to move rapidly away from the cannon fire. With the storm, each vessel now desperately needed those anchors to prevent them from drifting ashore.[17]

The storm raged all night, and on the morning of Thursday, July 12, the anchorage and shore showed the power of nature's fury. A couple of vessels were sunk, several had been driven ashore, and others dismasted. Hamond destroyed some of the beached and dismasted vessels for lack of materials, crew or time. The rapid expulsion from the island, the loss of much property, the bombardment of the island, and finally the storm, thoroughly demoralized the citizens of the floating town.[18]

To the south, the *Otter* still worked to free the flour ship, and late on Thursday, the ship floated free. Both vessels then anchored near Windmill Point. The *Lady Charlotte* still defiantly patrolled the waters of Hill's Bay between the *Otter* and the island. As the *Otter* and the flour ship sailed northward, the patriots felt complete victory.[19]

In June 1775, Royal Governor Dunmore had established the floating town, onboard the *Fowey* at Yorktown, in sight of southern Gloucester County. For thirteen months he had moved on the Chesapeake Bay at his discretion, slowly gathering strength. In July 1776, the patriots drove Dunmore from Gwynn's Island on the northern edge of Gloucester County. As they entered Maryland's waters, Dunmore and his loyalist supporters became exiles.

8

Exiles

On Friday, July 12, the militia commander for lower St. Mary's County, Maryland, suddenly received reports of "a considerable number of ships and small vessels between Smith's Point and Point Lookout." Colonel Richard Barnes personally investigated and counted almost seventy vessels. Two small vessels from that fleet had washed ashore, and the militia captured five crew members. Barnes interrogated them and learned that the fleet contained Governor Dunmore and Governor Eden. He also learned that the two governors intended to seize St. George's Island. Barnes took immediate action. He stationed almost 300 militia along the shore, and he requested more men from Colonel Jeremiah Jordan, commander of militia for upper St. Mary's County. He also asked for additional help from Captain Rezin Beall's company at Drum Point. By midnight Saturday, Barnes had completed his defensive preparations and informed the Maryland Council of Safety of his actions. Barnes then learned that three of his five prisoners had smallpox.[1]

While Barnes deployed his militia, Hamond, Dunmore and Eden boarded the *Fowey* and reconnoitered the waters and shores from St. Mary's County to St. George's Island. Satisfied that no threat existed on St. George's Island, they brought the fleet to within three miles of the island. Hamond ordered the ship's gun crews and marines to practice their weapons. The *Roebuck*'s crew threw overboard empty casks and barrels. One by one the gun crews fired the ship's cannons at the floating targets. From the upper deck, the Marines did the same with their muskets. The firing, particularly the eighteen-pounders, frightened and intimidated nearby residents. The breezes were moderate and the sound of the cannon carried for miles. The residents of St. George's Island correctly guessed they were the site of an imminent British attack. Under cover of darkness early Monday morning, July 15, some of the island's residents fled. Soon after dawn, ten ships' boats from the fleet went ashore on St. George's Island with almost 200 men. The remaining residents fled when the first boats touched the beach. The boats returned to the fleet for more men. By noon, approximately 350 British soldiers, marines, and loyalists occupied the island.[2]

St. George's Island was even smaller and more poorly situated than Gwynn's Island. A 100-yard-wide channel separated it from the Maryland shore. The channel was shallow and easily forded. The British began filling their water casks from the island's three wells while patrols searched the island. They found a few sheep and pigs. Meanwhile the Maryland militia concentrated its forces on the mainland opposite the island. To discourage harassment by the militia, the British sent a large row galley to cruise the shoreline.

While at Gwynn's Island, Hamond foresaw the need to develop a vessel to carry troops protected against musket fire and capable of clearing a beachhead to land. On Gwynn's Island, Hamond found the old hull of the snow *Fortune*, driven ashore in 1769, and rebuilt it into a row galley. Ship's carpenters cut the hull down and planked up the sides to protect the galley's oarsmen and occupants. The galley now drew less than two feet. Ship's carpenters mounted a six-pound cannon on a sliding carriage in the bow. Five swivel guns sat atop the frames along the galley's sides. As many as ten oarsmen could sit on each side of the galley protected behind the planking. Hamond sent the just completed galley to Montague the same day the troops landed on St. George's. Montague put the galley to use immediately.[3]

The galley proved a formidable weapon and had the desired effect on the militia. At dawn on Tuesday, July 16, the galley rowed close to the Maryland shoreline and for an hour kept up a continuous and heavy fire on the militia. "Their shot raked the ground on every part where the Men (militia) were stationed." The galley presented a difficult target to the militia since, behind the planking, "not a man (was) to be seen." However some of the militia's shots penetrated the galley's few exposed places. British midshipmen Brice was seriously wounded in the morning's action and died the next day. The British, despite Brice's loss, were pleased with the galley's potential and repeated the action that same afternoon. The galley rowed between the island and the mainland and, for two hours, kept up a continuous fire on the militia at close range. While under fire from the galley, the Maryland militia watched almost 300 British troops embark from the fleet, march over the island to a point opposite the militia, and then fire volley after volley at the militia from the island. A musket ball dangerously wounded militia Captain Rezin Beall who had arrived from Drum Point only the day before. At dusk, the galley and British troops withdrew.[4]

Colonel Jordan seriously considered moving his militia as much as half a mile inland due to the galley's strength. Jordan also reported the false rumor that the British were building a second row galley. Muskets seemed ineffective against the galley. To attack it as well as the troops on the island, Jordan needed cannon and swivel guns. The next day the British repeated the pattern—they landed each morning and withdrew each night while the galley patrolled the Narrows. By Thursday, July 18, it was obvious, however, the British did not intend to permanently occupy the island. Deserters from the fleet confirmed the British sought only water and wood and soon intended to leave the Bay. One of these deserters was loyalist James Cunningham, a bookkeeper for the Jameson Company of Norfolk. Cunningham's lengthy interrogation on July 18th by the Maryland Council of Safety provided accurate and detailed information on the British fleet's intent as well as the evacuation of Gwynn's Island. Based on his report and others, the Maryland militia determined their forces were sufficient to confront Dunmore's troops. The council even sent some militia from St. Mary's County to other areas of Maryland.[5]

Hamond was anxious to get to sea and the voyage to Maryland was only part of that process. Preparations for sea failed to meet Hamond's expectations. The water supply on St. George's proved inadequate, and he ordered Lt. John Orde to expedite loading of the fleet's transports with all available empty water casks. Hamond next planned a British raid up the Potomac to obtain water and necessary supplies for the return voyage. The raid awaited the loading of the water casks aboard the two transports. Once filled with water, the casks would be redistributed among the fleet. Orde returned from the transports late July 18 and informed Hamond that another full day's work was necessary. Orde also told him that Dunmore wanted to go on the raid. Hamond became angry at the news. He wrote Dunmore that the transport's master would be removed if under his (Hamond's) command. Indirectly, Hamond criticized Dunmore's leadership in this task. He asked Dunmore to apply pressure to the situation as "it is necessary to strain every nerve to its utmost in prosecuting the war." As to Dunmore's request to accompany the raid, Hamond politely suggested that if Dunmore for some reason could not go then Captain Leslie of the 14th could take his place. Hamond reflected bitterly that the "disgrace of (the) Gwynn's Island evacuation hangs so much about me." Dunmore's command of the 14th while at Gwynn's Island had not met Hamond's expectations.[6]

Dunmore knew Hamond wanted to command the 14th and that his role as governor interfered with normal military protocols. Nonetheless, while in Virginia, Hamond deferred to Dunmore's authority. Now they prepared to leave Virginia. Acutely aware of his increasingly precarious command authority, Dunmore knew his only chance to reestablish his authority in Virginia rested with Clinton's expedition. Clinton had told both Dunmore and Hamond in March that Virginia would receive his support. News of the disaster at Charleston had not yet arrived, and Dunmore still nurtured the hope that Clinton would help reestablish his rule as governor.

On Friday, July 19, the *Roebuck*, *Dunmore*, the row galley, three tenders and the two transports *Anna* and *William*, got underway up the Potomac River. The small but powerful fleet caused considerable alarm. Militia from both Maryland and Virginia assembled and shadowed the fleet from both sides of the Potomac. The fleet moved slowly and anchored near Herring Creek. At noon on Saturday, July 20th, the small fleet again set sail. Clouds moved in rapidly and the fleet anchored at dusk near Nomini Bay.

At dawn Sunday, the fleet got underway and anchored at 10 a.m. off Nanjemoy Creek just above Cedar Point. The row galley went into the creek and seized three local ferry boats. At 11 a.m. the fleet began to move, but the wind died and they again dropped anchor. By mid-afternoon the wind returned, and the fleet got underway. As they moved upriver, the *Roebuck* received information of a patriot militia gathering at a house on Nanjemoy Creek. On Hamond's orders the *Roebuck*'s lower deck 18-pound cannon fired several rounds in the direction of the house. They anchored after dark near Smith's Point. The next morning, thunderstorms accompanied the fleet to Sandy Point where they anchored at 4 p.m. in Mallows Bay. The weather moderated and working parties went ashore to fill the water casks. The watering operation continued well into the early morning.[7]

On the 22nd the fleet moved downriver off Acquia Creek in Virginia's Stafford County. The port of Dumfries lay two miles upriver in Virginia. The tenders sailed to both Cixamuxen Creek and Mattawonan Creek in Maryland opposite Dumfries looking for more water. Gradually, the transport's water casks were filled. By early Tuesday morning, July 23, the transports completed watering. So far the fleet had encountered little harassment from the militia. However, almost one hundred Stafford County militia gathered at the plantation of William Brent on the Virginia shore opposite the fleet. In Maryland, over three hundred militia under Colonel Benjamin Harrison guarded the shoreline. With Hamond's water-gathering mission complete, Dunmore sought action.[8]

With little time for rest, just before noon on that same Tuesday, Virginia's Royal Governor led his last raid on his colony. Two tenders escorted eight ships' boats and the row galley to the Virginia shore. They carried a force of 108 men. These included elements of the Queen's Own Loyal Virginians, Dunmore's Royal Ethiopians, the 14th Regiment and marines from the *Roebuck*—all led by Lord Dunmore. The row galley led the boats and fired several rounds of grapeshot at the assembled militia. The militia fired as the British landed but retreated before Dunmore could form ranks. Some British troops briefly pursued the retreating colonists. The British searched for supplies and then burned Brent's large brick home, outbuildings and haystacks. While

Dunmore contemplated his next direction of attack, the nearby Prince William militia hurried to attack Dunmore. The *Roebuck*'s lookouts spotted the militia's approach, and Hamond hoisted a white flag to signal Dunmore to return to the fleet. Bolstered by the approach of their fellow militia the Stafford County militia regrouped and began to fire on the British as they boarded their boats. Total casualties on both sides numbered at least fifteen, of which approximately half were killed. The boats returned to the fleet. Both sides claimed victory.[9]

In the late afternoon of July 23, Hamond sent the row galley directly to the Maryland shore and intimidated a large group of militia. The militia retreated without firing a shot. The galley's crew shouted at the departing militia and "called them sundry names." The galley touched the Maryland shore long enough to seize a small boat. They then fired the galley's six-pounder at the nearby home of a Mr. Fendall. The galley returned to the *Roebuck* and the fleet got underway down the Potomac.[10]

On July 24th, a small boat allegedly "with 3 of General Washington's servants" joined the British. The weather turned very bad, and the river's navigation became more difficult. The next day, the *Dunmore* ran aground off Upper Cedar Point, and it took eight hours to get her free. The following day the transport *William*, deeply laden with fresh water, ran aground near Leader's Ferry. Hamond acted quickly and got the *William* free. The unlucky *William* again ran aground a few hours later. Again, Hamond got her free in a matter of hours. At eight that night, in light winds, the fleet anchored near St. Clement's Island. The winds remained light through the night and next morning. Finally, at 1 p.m. on Saturday, July 27, Hamond got the fleet underway but sailed only as far as Ragged Point Island in the light winds. They anchored there just before midnight.[11]

While Dunmore and Hamond found water and diversion on the Potomac, the situation at St. George's Island deteriorated. The patriots knew from deserters that the British would leave as soon as the *Roebuck* and others returned. As the days wore on, however, the patriots grew impatient at the continued British presence and their own inactivity. Four cannon arrived for the Maryland militia between the 21st and 24th—a three-pounder, 2 four-pounders and a nine-pounder. The militia began building fortifications opposite the island and at nearby Cherryfields Point.[12]

Very early Thursday morning, July 25, one hundred militia crossed from the Maryland shore to St. George's Island. By dawn they had quietly moved across the island and lay in wait for the daily arrival of the fleet's water detail. The detail arrived on schedule but discovered the poorly concealed militia. The British dropped the empty water casks and fled back to the boats. The militia fired at the party, wounded several, and took one seaman prisoner. The *Fowey* investigated the shooting as the boats rowed swiftly back to the fleet. As soon as the *Fowey* learned of the ambush, Captain Montague ordered four of his nine-pounders fired at the island. The militia remained long enough to destroy the water casks and pollute the best of the island's three wells. Then they retreated across the Narrows to the mainland. While not an overwhelming success, the militia had taken the offensive.[13]

That afternoon, the militia learned that the Maryland State Navy ship *Defence* planned to attack the fleet. The *Defence* acted under the assumption that the *Roebuck* was still up the Potomac, and only the *Fowey* guarded the floating town. In size and armament the *Defence* nominally matched the *Fowey*. Whether or not the attack would succeed, it was an aggressive plan of action by the Marylanders. The militia learned of the return of the *Roebuck* at the same time they heard of the *Defence*'s plans. Riders were dispatched to warn the *Defence* of the changed situation, but they failed to locate the Maryland ship. The militia also mounted all four cannon on the mainland with the intention of disabling the *Fowey*. The main battery at Cherryfields Point was reinforced by militia.[14]

Militia Major Thomas Price developed an elaborate plan to attack the fleet. He positioned men on the shore and in small boats. He placed batteries to bring the *Fowey* under fire. On the afternoon of July 27, the *Defence* moved into the St. Mary's River to attack the *Fowey*. Montague ordered his crews to place anchors around the vessel and rig "springs." In the light airs, this allowed the *Fowey* to turn more reliably and at will, rather than by dependence on the wind. It also meant the crew stayed below decks and could either work the anchor ropes or man the guns. To attempt maneuver under sail exposed the crew to higher casualties and further tasked the reduced and weakened crew. As the *Fowey* prepared to meet the *Defence*, the battery at Cherryfields Point opened fire on the *Fowey*. Cannonballs from the nine-pounders hit a boat at the *Fowey*'s stern and hulled the warship. Almost simultaneously, the returning *Roebuck* sailed into sight of the *Fowey* and *Defence*. The *Defence* halted her advance, dropped anchor and reevaluated the changed British strength. Almost ten miles separated the *Defence* and the *Roebuck*.[15]

The next day the *Roebuck*, which feared nothing on the Chesapeake Bay, got underway and bore down on the *Defence* and her two escorts. A fresh breeze soon reached the *Fowey*, and she also got underway for the *Defence*. The *Defence* and her tenders made full sail for Point Lookout and the Chesapeake Bay. The *Fowey* was old and a dull sailor. During the chase, she lost her foretopmast. The *Roebuck* was new but so large that she needed a gale-force wind to sail her best. In the prevailing wind the Bay-built *Defence* easily outran the British and by 7, they gave up pursuit and anchored off St. George's Island. At 10 p.m. the *Roebuck* spotted two sails which proved to be the *Otter* and her tender.[16]

Hamond rejoined the fleet early on July 29. The transports had arrived the day before, but they were shadowed at a safe distance by two patriot row galleys. The British found themselves on the defensive. Water distribution to the fleet began immediately. On the 30th, Hamond ordered the *Otter* and *Fincastle* to cruise off the Virginia capes. Dunmore encouraged the private loyalist vessels to leave the fleet. Few felt compelled to stay.[17]

The process of culling the fleet's unseaworthy or poorly manned vessels began again. After Hamond's return, more than twenty vessels were beached, scuttled or burned. The Marylanders, like the Virginians, began to find dead bodies washed ashore. As at Gwynn's Island the corpses died of disease, not battle. The militia wrote that they were "poisoned with the stench." The summer heat and humidity increased the fleet's casualties from disease. Vessels left daily. By July 31st, over forty vessels had sailed south to rendezvous at the Virginia Capes. From there they eventually sailed to St. Augustine, New York, England or Scotland.[18]

In the raid on Brent's home, Dunmore found several newspaper accounts of the British fiasco at Charleston. He assumed the defeat probably changed Clinton's plans and certainly minimized the probability of support for of Dunmore's campaign. The *Otter*, stationed at the Capes, sought information from Clinton. Dunmore wrote Germain on July 31 and his anxiety about the future was evident. Dunmore agreed with Hamond to sail from the Chesapeake but,

> where we are to go, or what we can do next, to render service to his Majesty, I own I am puzzled to know, and I find there is now not even a chance of our receiving any assistance. I really am at a loss . . .

Still, Dunmore wrote Germain that he intended to harass and distress the rebels to the best of his ability. Dunmore sent his twenty-eight prisoners-of-war aboard the *Otter* for Captain Squires to deliver to Governor Tonyn in St. Augustine. Dunmore wrote Tonyn that he had wanted them to be exchanged "but the Rebels have ever avoided it." Hamond ordered Squires to take the prisoners as well as escort loyalist vessels to St. Augustine. Squires was then to return "without loss of time" to the Virginia Capes. From the *Dunmore*'s cabin, as he wrote Germain, the Governor could see Montague's seamen burning the condemned vessels.[19]

Thursday, August 1, began with thunder and lightning. Hamond sent naval crews on board various vessels to insure their readiness for sea. The preparations took all day. The next morning, the *Fowey* gave the signal to make sail. Even with reduced numbers, it took over two hours to get the ravaged fleet underway. The *Roebuck* remained behind while her crew completed destruction of a few unseaworthy vessels and secured the rear of the fleet from attack. Strong winds moved the fleet quickly down the Bay. As they passed Point Lookout, the *Roebuck*'s tender, *Pembroke*, arrived from the south with news.[20]

Shortly after 6 p.m. the fleet anchored off Tangier Island. That night, Hamond and Dunmore read the *Pembroke*'s dispatches of the British expedition at Charleston. Letters from Parker and Clinton recounted the fiasco and advised Dunmore that they were now unable to support a Virginia campaign. This news ended any possibility of a campaign by Dunmore to retake Virginia. He wrote another note to Germain. The lack of Clinton's

Figure 13 Potomac River Operations

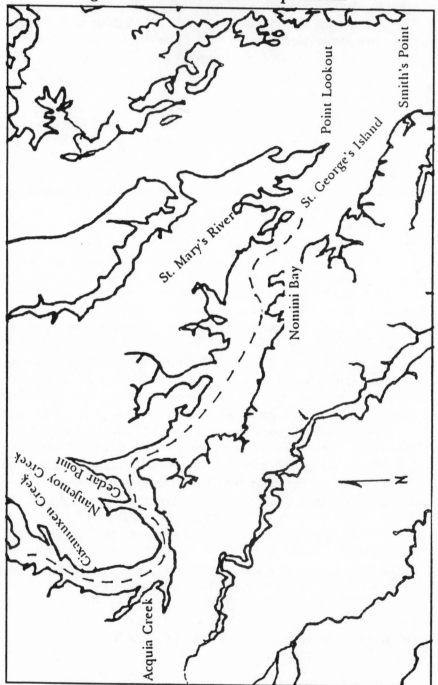

Figure 14 Exodus of the Floating Town

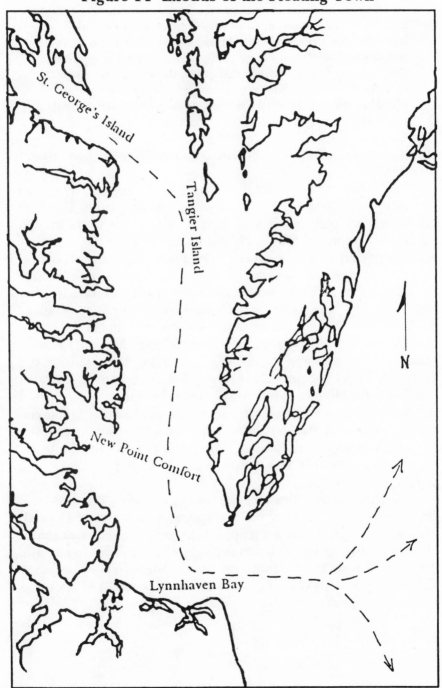

support,

> will render my Situation (if possible) more intolerable than it
> has been for these fourteen Months past, that I have been
> constantly pened (sic) up in a ship hardly with the common
> Necessaries of life, but what makes it a thousand times worse,
> in that I am left without even the hope of being able to render
> His Majesty the smallest Service, this I must say is truly
> discouraging . . .

Dunmore's role as Royal Governor of Virginia was almost
finished.[21]

Early the next morning, Saturday, August 3, Hamond
removed the cannon from the row galley and scuttled it. The fleet
got underway and by evening passed New Point Comfort. On
Sunday morning the fleet anchored in Lynnhaven Bay. Another
assessment of the fleet's readiness took place. As a result Hamond
burned and destroyed another dozen vessels. At noon on Sunday
the floating town numbered barely sixty vessels and most in poor
condition. That afternoon the *Otter* sailed with over forty vessels to
St. Augustine. It included Dunmore's patriot prisoners.[22]

On Sunday, with the fleet reduced to less than twenty vessels,
Hamond ordered some apple cider sent to the *Pembroke* from the
Susannah, a recent prize. The *Fowey* sailed the following day with
seven vessels. Montague followed Hamond's orders and escorted
the vessels about twenty-four miles offshore. While Montague
performed escort duty, Hamond ordered Whitworth and the
Pembroke to cruise between the Virginia Capes. When Montague
returned, Whitworth was to place himself under Montague's
orders.[23]

Hamond made final preparations to sail. The *Roebuck*,
Dunmore, *William*, *Anna*, three transports, and seven other small
vessels remained. Hamond stripped the prize vessel *Susannah* of
her remaining cargo and serviceable items. In addition to the
cider, the Rhode Island sloop contained rum, cheese, shoes, soap
and chocolate. This valuable cargo was distributed by Hamond as
he thought appropriate. By Tuesday evening August 6, Hamond
and Dunmore agreed to take the remaining fleet to New York.
Hamond listed the reasons as,

1st The total impracticability of rendering his Majesty any services by remaining, with the very few Men we had left capable of doing duty.

2d The impossibility of landing even to water the ships (the springs on the Islands being all dried up).

3d The necessity of the Admiral & General's being acquainted with our situation as soon as possible, to prevent the disgrace His Majestys Troops might suffer when their extream (sic) weakness became known to the Enemy.

Just before departing Virginia, Hamond wrote his good friend Hans Stanley, Governor of the Isle of Wight,

The history of a defensive kind of war, which has been my misfortune for some time past to have been engaged in, is painful for me to relate, and would give you no pleasure to read. In short, the support & protection that I have been under the absolute necessity of giving Lord Dunmore & his floating town . . . has given full employment for three ships, for these three months past, to prevent them from falling into the hands of the Enemy. . . . However, this inconvenience is now nearly at an end.

On Wednesday, August 7, Hamond, Dunmore and the last remnants of the floating town sailed to New York to join Clinton.[24]

For over fourteen months, the Chesapeake Bay had been dominated and threatened by Dunmore's presence. Now he, the loyalists, the troops, and the Royal Navy were gone. Yet Dunmore never lost complete hope that he would again rule Virginia. His appointment as governor and his subsequent exile became an obsession. Hamond concluded in his later narrative that as he left the Virginia Capes in August 1776, he "ended my command to the Southward." The *Virginia Gazette* on Saturday, August 10, 1776 featured a story about the final exodus of the British. The *Gazette*'s editor offered its readers the hope, "May they never return."[25]

George Washington's wife Martha, who remained in Virginia throughout most of the American Revolution, wrote to her friend Mercy Warren in 1778. Although two years had elapsed since Dunmore's departure, Martha still recalled her feelings and those of many patriots about their last Royal Governor. Martha wrote Mercy of the improved conditions in Virginia "since the cruel Dunmore left us."[26]

9

Epilogue

By August 8, 1776 the last vestiges of royal authority in Virginia and Maryland disappeared over the horizon. Less than a month earlier the British had retreated from Gwynn's Island.

The *Santa Barbara* with Captain Gomalez and Mr. Eduardo sailed for Bermuda. Their mainmast finally split, and, in a defenseless condition, they were boarded by the Continental Navy vessel *Lexington*. Fortunately, the Americans honored Dunmore's British pass as well as Spanish neutrality. The *Santa Barbara* limped into St. George's, Bermuda on August 21 and returned home to Hispaniola on October 22. The Spanish government exonerated Eduardo for the loss of the silver. The Spaniards shared their observation of American successes and British defeats. The British, however, kept all the Spaniard's 12,500 pesos.[1]

The Americans buried the Frenchman, Captain Arundel, near his battery commanding Gwynn's Island. Two French prisoners captured by Dunmore, the Chevalier de St. Aubin and the Chevalier de Harcourt, found passage back home and praised the American success.[2]

Acting Captain Charles Harrison rose to command one of the four Continental Regiments of Artillery. Harrison's 1st Continental Artillery Regiment served throughout the war, in the Chesapeake, Philadelphia, Charleston, the Carolinas and Yorktown. All of the Virginia regiments that served at Gwynn's Island, the 1st Virginia Regiment of Foot, 2nd Virginia Regiment of Foot, 7th Virginia Regiment of Foot and elements of the 3rd, 4th, 5th, 6th and 8th served in the Continental line throughout the war.[3]

Brigadier General Andrew Lewis was passed over in Continental promotions to Major General a year after Gwynn's Island. He subsequently resigned his Continental commission due to health but continued as a militia commander. He died in 1781. Major Andrew Leitch died of wounds received in the battles around New York in October 1776. Colonel James Hendricks eventually commanded the 1st Virginia Regiment after Colonel William Daingerfield resigned. Colonel Hugh Mercer was promoted to Brigadier General and died of wounds received at Princeton. Colonel William Woodford, who commanded the Americans in Norfolk in 1775-1776, died while a prisoner-of-war in November 1780.[4]

The British loyalist units barely survived the war. The Queen's Own Loyal Virginia Regiment lost its Colonel, Jacob Ellegood, before the Gwynn's Island campaign. When the fleet disintegrated, so did the regiment. Dunmore's Royal Ethiopian Regiment fared no better. Elements of both the Queens and the Ethiopians accompanied Dunmore to New York after leaving Virginia in August 1776. They joined the regular British and other loyalist units there. At least six of the Ethiopians were still in New York when the British evacuated the city in 1783.[5]

The last loyalist unit Dunmore created but which never served at Gwynn's Island was the Loyal Foresters under Colonel John Connolly, M.D. Connolly served Dunmore's interests in the western part of the colony. He was captured in November 1775 and imprisoned for almost five years. He rejoined the British in New York and was reinstated as Colonel by Sir Henry Clinton. He recruited the Loyal Foresters from loyalists in New York, Virginia and North Carolina and served under Cornwallis in the British southern campaign. Connolly surrendered with Cornwallis at Yorktown.[6]

Governor Robert Eden of Maryland went back to England in the supply ship *Levant*. He was a young man but not well. Eden suffered from dropsy, a condition which gradually weakens its victims through excess of lymphatic fluids. A grateful King knighted Eden for his service in America. As governor of Maryland from 1767 until 1776 Eden had skillfully walked the middle ground between the coercive policies of the crown and the colonists' demands. After the signing of the Peace of Paris in 1783, Eden returned to Maryland and made claims for compensation. In Annapolis, he not only pressed his own claims but entered several dozen new claims. A dispute arose over the claims' validity. They were signed and dated when Eden was Maryland's Royal Governor but no record of them existed and "the ink was fresh." Eden contracted a fever while in Annapolis. On September 2, 1784, Robert Eden succumbed to dropsy and died at a friend's house on Shipwright Street. He was buried in St. Margaret's Churchyard on the Severn River. He was only 43 years old. The former governor's claims were set aside.[7]

Virginia Governor John Murray, Lord Dunmore, never lost his enthusiasm to prosecute the war and improve his personal fortune, but his opportunities were limited. He left Virginia in August 1776, and went to New York with Hamond. When the reduced fleet arrived off Staten Island on Tuesday, August 13, an American prisoner, Captain Hunter, escaped and informed Washington of Dunmore's arrival. Washington was unimpressed. Dunmore's remaining effectives numbered less than 150 and unwittingly introduced smallpox and yellow fever to the British garrison in New York. Washington already faced 22,000 British. Hamond's ragged fleet of 14 vessels joined the over 330 British vessels in New York. The following evening, August 14, Admiral Richard Howe hosted thirty-four for dinner aboard his flagship *Eagle*, 64 guns. Lord Dunmore dined with Admiral Howe, Lord Cornwallis, Sir Peter Parker, Commodore Hotham, General Heister, Lord Percy, General Grant, Admiral Shuldham, Sir William Erskine, General William Howe—the Admiral's brother— and others. "They all expressed great Satisfaction at their Entertainment."[8]

Amid this wealth of British resources, Dunmore pursued anew his scheme to retake Virginia. However, British attention was focused on the capture of New York. In the Battle of Long Island on August 26, Dunmore served with the Highlanders and Hessian mercenaries. His role was minor but distinguished. He always exhibited personal bravery in combat. The remnants of Ethiopians also fought on Long Island. One of the few captured British prisoners was "Major Cudjo, commander of Lord Dunmore's black regiment." After New York fell on September 16, Dunmore renewed his request for troops and ships for a Virginia campaign. While he awaited Clinton's favor Dunmore and other British officers moved into comfortable quarters in the city. From his residence on Broadway, Dunmore witnessed the huge fire in late September which destroyed 493 homes. While British didn't set the fire, Dunmore's presence and the burning of Norfolk created an air of suspicion. Dunmore came close to his goal for support, but by early November Dunmore decided to return to England.[9]

With New York secure, Howe intended to return many of the British troops to England. He selected the *Fowey* as one of the convoy vessels. On November 12, 1776 the *Fowey*, with Dunmore aboard, sailed for England. Some loyalists who had accompanied the governor to New York stayed there, but others returned with Dunmore to England. In England Dunmore resumed his seat in the House of Lords and worked with other loyalists to press claims for lost property in America. The King generously continued his governor's salary of £2,000 annually, with a supplemental payment annually of £1,000 through the war. In addition, he received a draw of £15,000 on whatever claims settlement might be made someday, if the British lost the colonies.[10]

In 1777, Dunmore proposed recruitment of 4,000 Scots for an expedition to America with himself as Colonel. The King overruled the plan. Finally, in April 1781, Dunmore received permission to raise a military force to reestablish a royal government in Virginia. Cornwallis's army approached Virginia and a favorable outcome there was anticipated. Dunmore's support included two transports, large siege cannon, small arms and other necessary supplies. Loyalists in England on pensions formed the bulk of his military force. Those pensioners who failed to join Dunmore's Virginia expedition would forfeit their pensions. Among his company were John Grymes, James Ingram, John Brown and other Virginians in exile. Dunmore's expedition included the transports *Laurie* and *Juliana*. He sailed from England in October 1781, aboard the *Rotterdam*, and he arrived at British held Charleston on December 21, 1781. He was well received by the town's loyalists. At Charleston, Dunmore learned of Cornwallis' surrender at Yorktown. Dunmore, ever the opportunist, refused to give up his expedition.[11]

Dunmore remained in Charleston and continued to advance

new schemes for use of his military forces. Initially Clinton supported him. He wrote Dunmore at Charleston "for next to Lord Cornwallis . . . there is none so able to form and execute so great a design nor in whom the King's friends have equal confidence as in your Lordship." A prominent South Carolina loyalist, John Cruden, proposed raising an army of 10,000 blacks. Dunmore's experience with the Royal Ethiopians and Cruden's support encouraged the ambitious Governor. On March 30, 1782 Dunmore sailed on the *Carysfort* in a large convoy to British held New York and advanced the idea to Clinton. Dunmore also suggested a base be established at both Old Point Comfort and Sewell's Point in Virginia to control commerce. The Governor's ideas were militarily sound. Rumors of Dunmore's schemes reached the French commander in Virginia, Rochambeau. He seriously worried about an invasion by Dunmore. Clinton, however, was now lukewarm to the idea of prosecuting the war.[12]

Within a month of Dunmore's arrival in New York, Sir Guy Carleton replace Clinton. Carleton's instructions from London specifically discouraged resumption of hostilities. Dunmore realized that he might now only expect support in England. He sailed to England and lobbied from May to October of 1782. Dunmore also advanced a plan to have loyalists independently conquer the Mississippi River basin. Even though Dunmore still enjoyed considerable patronage, the crown supported none of Dunmore's ventures.[13]

In 1784, Dunmore was reelected to the House of Lords. He continued to use his influence to press loyalist claims and, along with former Governors Eden of Maryland and Galloway of Pennsylvania, led the loyalist lobby group. In 1787, King George III appointed Dunmore Royal Governor of the Bahamas. Dunmore left England on August 28, 1787 and remained in the Bahamas until 1797. Although he found many old loyalist friends from Virginia in the Bahamas, he ran into problems. His arrogance and arbitrary rule created complaints, and charges against him went back to London. Coincident with the complaints' arrival in England, two serious setbacks for Dunmore occurred. Prime Minister Pitt realigned the cabinet and caused Earl Gower, Marquis of Stafford, to resign. In addition to being Dunmore's brother-in-law, Gower had consistently been one of Dunmore's strongest and most influential patrons. Far worse for Dunmore, his daughter Augusta secretly married Prince Augustus Frederick, a younger son of King George III. This violated the Royal Marriage Act and the King's wrath was great.[14]

In 1796, the King dismissed Dunmore as Governor, and he returned home the following spring. With little patronage or favor, Dunmore retired to the seaside resort of Ramsgate in Kent, England. He died there at Southwood House on February 25, 1809 at the age of 77. His wife died there on November 11, 1818. Both were buried at St. Lawrence on the Isle of Thanet, Kent.[15]

Of all the principals at Gwynn's Island, the floating town's Commodore survived the longest. Captain Andrew Snape Hamond continued command of the *Roebuck* until 1780. General William Howe and Admiral Richard Howe sought Hamond's experience to determine a route to attack Philadelphia. Hamond knew well both the Chesapeake Bay and the Delaware River. He recommended the Delaware River route, but the Howes chose the Chesapeake. It failed. The Howes, particularly Richard, had long been Hamond's patrons, and he was ready to return the favor. In 1779, before a Parliamentary Review Committee, Hamond supported their choice of attack routes as appropriate to the situation.[16]

In December 1778, while in command of the *Roebuck*, Hamond had received a knighthood. The following spring, on March 7, he married Ann Graeme. In 1781, Hamond became Lieutenant-Governor of Nova Scotia, Commissioner of the Navy, and Commander-in-Chief of His Majesty Ships at Halifax. Halifax had become the primary British port in North America after the fall of Boston. Yet little had been done to systematically develop and organize Halifax's facilities. Hamond provided the comprehensive planning and experience necessary to make the port efficient. He anticipated being made Governor of Nova Scotia, but the fall of Lord North's government in 1782, eliminated his chief sponsors. As consolation the King elevated Hamond to a baronet in late 1783.[17]

The end of the American Revolution placed Hamond on half pay. In 1785 he hoisted his flag as Commodore in the *Irresistible*, 74 guns, and he served as Commander-in-Chief of the large naval facilities in the River Medway and at the Nore. This post was primarily "shore duty" and assured him of a substantial income.

The outbreak of the Wars of the French Revolution in 1792 again brought experienced captains into active naval service. Hamond was posted as second in command of the Channel Fleet under Viscount Hood. Unfortunately, Hamond's health was poor, and at 53, he found sea duty difficult. In 1793, he was made Extra Commissioner on the Navy Board, and in 1794 Deputy Comptroller of the Navy. Within the year, Hamond received promotion to Comptroller of the Navy. He held the post until 1806 when Prime Minister Pitt died. While in that post, Hamond participated in the Admiralty reforms initiated by the Earl St. Vincent. In 1796, he successfully stood for Parliament for Ispwich. In 1806, he retired near Lynn, Norfolk. That Christmas season his only son, Captain Graham Eden Hamond, married. Andrew Hamond lived to see his son made a Rear-Admiral in 1825. On September 21, 1828, Andrew Snape Hamond died at home in Lynn at the age of 89. His son later became a Vice-Admiral in 1837, Admiral in 1847 and later served as Admiral of the Fleet.[18]

The events of May, June, and July 1776 changed Gwynn's Island. With the departure of Dunmore and Hamond in July, some Virginia troops pursued them to Maryland while most joined General Washington's Army at New York. Several companies remained on the island into the fall of 1776 as garrison troops. The hasty departure of the British left much on and around the island. These included at least 18 anchors on the bottom of Hill's Bay. Kingston Parish resident Samuel Eden leased two schooners from island resident Stapleton Keeble. Eden built a device to locate and raise the anchors. He recovered 17 anchors, some chain and much rope. Most of the recovered equipment went to the Virginia State Navy. The largest anchor went to Baltimore and was placed aboard the Continental Frigate *Virginia* (28 guns). Captain James Nicholson, formerly of the Maryland *Defence*, eventually commanded the *Virginia*. Eden's salvage operations in August and September of 1776 provided some diversion for the garrison troops.[19]

The British occupation of the east end of the island and the quarantined area discouraged resettlement by the Gwynns. Humphrey Gwynn offered the property and dwellings for sale. Eventually, the area became known as the Hill's Plantation. During the seven week occupation, the British deforested much of the island. Troop movements, herds of animals, and earthwork construction also exposed vast amounts of soil. Together the deforestation and massive soil disturbance caused much erosion. It took years to restore the island's agricultural productivity.[20]

Across the Haven, similar activities by the patriots affected property there. When the patriot troops first arrived from Williamsburg to oppose the British, they tore down several homes in the line of fire. Daniel Marchant, Elisha Marchant, Henry Powell, Philip Reed, Joseph Shipley and Ralph Shipley lost their homes. They eventually received compensation from the state for those losses. The patriot garrison troops removed much evidence of the occupation. By October 1776, all remaining Continental troops were withdrawn from the island and county. Only the militia remained in the area.[21]

Sir John Peyton served throughout the Revolution as the Gloucester County Lieutenant. He assigned John Billups' company to patrol the Kingston Parish region. Billups used foot patrols, canoes and horses to patrol the parish's extensive shoreline. In July 1776 the powerful sailing galley *Henry* entered for the Virginia State Navy. The galley was built in Kingston Parish on the East River. Her captain, Robert Tompkins, recruited much of the crew from Kingston Parish and Gloucester County. From 1776 to 1779 the *Henry* patrolled the coast between the York and Rappahannock Rivers.[22]

Gwynn's Island resumed commercial activity in 1777. The island's shipbuilding activity and resources were severely damaged as a result of the occupation. It took almost a year to restore that industry. In October 1777, the small 15-ton schooner *Whim* sailed from Gwynn's Island. She was registered at Port Norfolk on the Elizabeth River. Her owners were John Gwynn, William Gwynn, Samuel Davies and Samuel Eastwood. The crew came from Kingston Parish, but the captain, William Gregory, was a Bostonian. The vessel made at least two voyages to the West Indies. The *Whim*'s last voyage left Norfolk in August 1778 and arrived at St. Thomas less than two weeks later. There the *Whim* took a cargo of rum, sugar and dry goods. On her return to Virginia on October 8, the British privateer *Lord Howe* captured the *Whim* just south of Cape Henry. The British captain, Thomas

John, took the *Whim* to New York where an Admiralty Court awarded the vessel to the British. The loss hurt the island's recovery. By 1778, other vessels served the island's trade but the threats to commerce centered on loyalist activities in the Bay.[23]

The former Kingston Parish loyalist, John Wilkie, returned to the Chesapeake in 1779 as captain of the British privateer *Sutherland*. The *Sutherland* and two other British privateers cooperated with two Royal Navy vessels in operations against patriot shipping. Wilkie and his associates cruised the Potomac, Rappahannock, the Piankatank, and around Gwynn's Island. With Wilkie's knowledge of local waters, the loyalists and their Royal Navy allies easily seized several vessels while they avoided capture. Wilkie also briefly saw his old estate on Queen's Creek. By 1780 Wilkie was in New York, and after the war, he went to Canada.[24]

In the winter of 1779-1780 the Chesapeake Bay froze over solid as far south as New Point Comfort. The ice halted much traffic on the Bay. In 1781 Lord Cornwallis invaded Virginia. He reconnoitered Hampton Roads for a base of operations but chose instead to situate his army at Yorktown. The Yorktown campaign halted overseas trade to and from the Bay between July 1781 and October 1781. The presence of the British at Yorktown encouraged loyalists to harass the patriots. One of the most prominent of these loyalists was Joseph Wheland.[25]

During the Revolution Joseph Wheland, a Maryland loyalist, commanded a small fleet of schooners and rowing barges on the Chesapeake Bay. He operated from Tangier Sound and usually attacked the Eastern and Western shores of Maryland. On at least one occasion he attacked and seized a vessel near Gwynn's Island. In his flagship, *Rover*, he captured a forty-ton schooner anchored off Gwynn's Island in October of 1781. John Greenwood, the schooner's captain, was kept aboard as a prisoner and a mulatto captain named George commanded the prize crew of ten men. George took Greenwood's schooner a short distance up the Piankatank River. With the schooner secure, Wheland waited nearby in the *Rover* until dark, muffled his oars and rowed across Hill's Bay to Gwynn's Island "to rob one Mr. Gwynn." Wheland and half a dozen loyalists quickly went ashore and broke into Gwynn's warehouse on Edwards Creek. They removed the cargo Greenwood had "deposited" there which included a hogshead of rum. Wheland and his loyalists got safely away. During Wheland's raid Greenwood recaptured his schooner. In the struggle, several loyalists were killed, including one drowned in the Piankatank.[26]

Dunmore incessantly complained that he lacked sufficient resources to successfully reconquer Virginia. However, opportunities had existed. Clinton's 1776 expedition, with 5,000 soldiers, 3,000 sailors and a huge fleet, initially had a better chance for success in Virginia than anywhere else. It was poor British intelligence that sent Clinton's campaign to Charleston instead. In 1776, both Dunmore and Clinton controlled the sea and moved without restraint. In 1781, British Lieutenant General Cornwallis, with only 9,000 soldiers and a small fleet, lost control of the sea briefly on two occasions. It doomed his army and the British efforts to retake the colonies.

In 1781, the French fleet under Compte DeGrasse confined Cornwallis to the Chesapeake Bay. A faint-hearted attempt by the British to dislodge DeGrasse's fleet failed. Cornwallis made an attempt to transport his forces across the York River from Yorktown to the British base in Gloucester County where loyalist forces, commanded by Lieutenant Colonel Banastre Tarleton, controlled the area. A storm arose which capsized some of the British transports and discouraged the rest. With his retreat blocked and no reinforcements, a besieged Cornwallis surrendered his army at Yorktown on October 18, 1781 in sight of Gloucester County. Effectively, that surrender ended the military phase of the American Revolution. Ironically, Yorktown and Gloucester County had also been the start and end of Lord Dunmore's campaign in Virginia.[27]

Gwynn's Island trade rebounded after Cornwallis' defeat. After 1781, the Gwynns used increasingly larger vessels to protect themselves against privateers and pirates. Trade with Dutch, French, Spanish, Danish and British ports in the West Indies continued until the Peace of Paris in 1783. The treaty closed most British ports and the West Indies to American trade. That restriction and the reduced post-war trade hurt Gwynn's Island's overseas commerce. The island's economy remained depressed until after 1790.

The occupation and seizure of Gwynn's Island resembled the American Revolution in miniature. The Gwynn's Island campaign contained British military units, loyalist forces, loyalist sympathizers, neutrals (Spanish and French), Continental Army units, State recruits, militia, a French military officer serving in the American Continental Army, and innocent civilians and their property. Among the loyalist units on Gwynn's Island was Dunmore's Royal Ethiopians, recruited from freed African Americans. Dunmore's resources and the forces which opposed him represented coalitions. The British prosecuted the American Revolution by use of a coalition of regular troops, loyalists, German mercenaries and naval forces. The Americans won the American Revolutionary War only through a coalition of Continental regular troops, State units, militia, French troops and French Naval forces.

Sea power sustained Dunmore's campaign, and the British generally enjoyed control of the sea throughout the American Revolution. Despite that control, Dunmore and the British suffered from poor communications. Letters from Britain arrived months after they were written and often did not accurately reflect changed political or military situations. Poor communications hampered British commanders in America throughout the Revolution. The communications issue ran deeper than timeliness or quantity. Dunmore's responsibility included the support of the policies of the British ministers and King George III. Dunmore executed strategy designed to maintain British sovereignty, yet he received little policy guidance to develop his strategy. Throughout the Revolution, an absence of defined, consistent British policy to pursue and win the American war, also hampered British strategy.

Dunmore suffered not only from the lack of coherent strategy but from his own personal arrogance. Dunmore displayed only contempt for the patriots and often discounted their strength and abilities. His methods and tactics frequently polarized those he encountered. His attitude toward and misuse of neutrals usually antagonized them toward him. Dunmore possessed considerable disdain for others, but Clinton, Burgoyne, Howe, and other British commanders frequently displayed a similar arrogance. The strategy and tactics Dunmore employed to intimidate and subdue Virginia produced the opposite effect. The harder Dunmore tried to control the Virginians, the more they sought freedom. The harder Dunmore attempted to reimpose royal authority, the more Virginians worked to develop their own government.

Appendix 1

Vessels of the Floating Town, May-August, 1776

NAME	TYPE (Cannon)	COMMANDER	FUNCTION
ADONIS	Brig (6)	Roberts, John	Hospital Ship
ADVENTURE			Private/ McAlisters
ANNA	Ship		Stores/Troops
BETSEY	Brig	Fenner, Mr.	Private/Fenner
BETSEY	Brig	Boyne, Capt.	Private/Boynes
BETSEY	Brig	Coakley, Dr.	Private/Coakley
BETSEY	Sloop	Kerr, Samuel	Private/Kerrs
CAMPBELL	Sloop	Farmer, Samuel	Private/Farmers
CHARLOTTE	Schooner	Hargraves, Wm.	Private/ Hargraves
CHRISTIE	Sloop	Avery, James	Private/Roberts & Sheddens
DOLPHIN	Brig	McAlister, Hector	Private/ McAlisters
DOLPHIN	Pilot Boat	James, Edward	Tender-*Roebuck*
DUNLUCE	Ship	Shutter, Robt.	Troopship
DUNMORE	Ship	Buchanan, John	Troopship

NAME	TYPE (Cannon)	COMMANDER	FUNCTION
DUNMORE (ex-Eilbeck)	Ship/ Frigate (6)	Lowes, James	Flagship
EDWARD	Sloop (6)	Boger, Lt. Richard	Tender-*Liverpool*
ELIZABETH	Brig		Supply ship
FANNY	Brig	McCaw, Dr.	Private/McCaws
FANNY	Schooner		Private/ Goodrichs
FINCASTLE	Brig	Jamieson, Neil	
FINCASTLE, HMS	Sloop (14)	Wright, Lt. John	Tender-*Otter*
FOWEY, HMS	Ship (24)	Montague, Capt. Geo.	Warship
FRIENDSHIP	Pilot Boat	Smith, Robert	Dispatch vessel
GAGE	Schooner		Tender-*Roebuck*
GALLEY	Row Galley	Brice, Midshipman	Warship
GRACE	Ship		Captured/Penn.
GRACE	Ship		Private/ Flemmings
HAMMOND	Ship	Hunter, John	Private/Sprowls & Hunters
HAMOND	Brig	Parker, James	
HELENA	Brig	Stewart, Roger	Prison Ship
JAMES	Sloop	Goodrich, Wm.	Privateer
JOHN	Sloop (4)		Tender
JOHN GRYMES	Sloop	Grymes, John	Troopship
KINGFISHER, HMS	Sloop (14)	Graeme, Alex.	Warship
LADY AUGUSTA	Sloop	Lowes, Capt.	Private
LADY CHARLOTTE	Schooner	Thomas, Mid.	Warship
LADY GAGE	Sloop		Tender-*Fowey*

NAME	TYPE (Cannon)	COMMANDER	FUNCTION
LADY GOWER	Schooner	Wilkie, John	Tender-*Dunmore*
LADY STANLEY	Schooner (2)	Younghusband, Wm.	Tender
LADY SUSAN	Sloop (6)	Goodrich, Wm.	Privateer
LADY SUSANNA	Schooner (6)	Goodrich, Bridger	Privateer
LEVANT	Ship	Thomas, Samuel	Storeship
LILLY	Sloop	Goodrich, John	Privateer
LIVELY, HMS	Frigate (20)		
LIVELY	Schooner		Privateer
LIVERPOOL, HMS	Frigate (28)	Bellew, Capt. Henry	Warship
LOGAN	Ship	Logan	Private/Logans
LORD HOWE	Sloop	Orde, 2nd Lt. John	Tender-*Roebuck*
LORD NORTH	Sloop (2)	MacDonald, Charles	Privateer
MARIA	Brig	Marshall, John Jr.	Storeship
MARIA	Sloop		Tender
MARIA	Brig	Allison, John	Private/Allisons
MOLLY	Ship	Ridley, James	Storeship
OTTER, HMS	Sloop (14)	Squire, Capt. Matthew	Warship
PEACE & PLENTY	Sloop	Eilbeck, Mr.	Private
PEGGY	Brig	Goodrich, John	Private/Goodrichs
PEMBROKE	Sloop (4)	Whitworth, Lt. Richard	Tender-*Roebuck*
POLLY	Brig	Robinson, James	Captured

NAME	TYPE (Cannon)	COMMANDER	FUNCTION
RANGER	Schooner	Philips, 3rd Lt., also James, Edward	Tender-*Roebuck*
REBECCA	Brig	Brown, John	Storeship
ROEBUCK, HMS	Frigate (44)	Hamond, Capt. A.S.	Flagship
SANTA BARBARA	Snow	Gomalez	Captured/ Spanish
SUSANNAH	Sloop	Remington, Peleg	Captured/R.I.
THOMAS	Schooner	Calderhead, Wm.	Private/ Calderhead
UNICORN	Snow	Wilkinson, James	Blacksmith Shop
Unknown	Schooner	Brown, John	Private/Browns
Unknown	Schooner	Leyburn, Peter	Storeship
Unknown	Ship	Wilson, Thos.	Storeship
Unknown	Sloop (10)	Stuart, Robt.	Privateer
Unknown	Sloop	Pickets, Mr.	Private/ Goodrich & Shedden
Unknown	Sloop	Gibson, Mr.	Private/ Goodrich & Shedden
Unknown	Sloop		Private/ Goodrich & Shedden
Unknown	Sloop		Private/ Goodrich & Shedden
Unknown	Sloop		Private/ Goodrich & Shedden
VULCAN	Sloop	Ingram, James	
WILLIAM	Ship (2)		Storeship/ Troops

NAME	TYPE (Cannon)	COMMANDER	FUNCTION
WILLIAM & ANNA	Brig		Hospital ship
WILLIAM & CHARLES	Brig		Storeship/Rum

The above represent all identified vessels from sources in the bibliography. Most contemporary accounts estimate the floating town's size at approximately 100 vessels. Specific reliable estimates range from 92 to 108, while others go as high as 132. Between late May and early July, 1776, 100 vessels represents a reliable estimate of the floating town's average size. The unlisted vessels were probably small sloops, schooners, pilot boats, and log canoes.

Appendix 2

Loyalists in the Floating Town, May-August, 1776

NAME	RESIDENCE	VOCATION
Agnew, James	Portsmouth	Merchant
Agnew, Stair	Virginia	QOLV
Aitcheson, Alexander	Norfolk	
Aitcheson, Dick	Norfolk	
Aitcheson, William	Norfolk	Merchant
Aitcheson, spouse (Wm.)	Norfolk	
Aitcheson, childen	Norfolk	
Alexander, Charles	Norfolk	
Allan, Adam	Virginia	
Allason, John	Norfolk	
Allason, spouse (John)	Norfolk	
Allason, children (John)	Norfolk	
Anbler, Lawrence		DRER
Anderson, Peter[2]	Norfolk	
Anderson, spouse[2] (Peter)	Norfolk	
Anderson, children[2] (Peter)	Norfolk	
Anderson, William		DRER
Armstead, William		DRER

NAME	RESIDENCE	VOCATION
Armston, Freer	Norfolk	Tallow chandler/soap boiler
Armston, spouse	Norfolk	
Armston, children	Norfolk	
Arnott, James		
Arwin, Samuel	Norfolk	Clerk to Farrar
Ashbridge, Christopher	Norfolk	Clerk to Farrar
Ashley, Quash		DRER
Atkinson, Mr.	Somerset Co., MD	
Austin, Brockenborough		
Barkley, Mr.	Somerset Co., MD	
Baynes, Elizabeth	Norfolk	
Baynes, John	Norfolk	
Baynes, Robert	Norfolk	Merchant
Bealey, Thomas	Baltimore	Master/pilot
Begg, John	Norfolk	Merchant
Bell, Margaret		
Biran, George		DRER
Blackburn, John	Norfolk	Clerk to Ingram
Blair, George	Norfolk	Merchant/QOLV, Capt.
Boush, Jenny[1]		
Boush, Jenny[1]		
Boush, Judith[1]		
Boush, Mary Bradley[1]		
Boush, Max[1]		
Boyd, John	Norfolk	Clerk to Farrar
Bradley, Mr.		Comptroller, Lower Dist. James River
Brittain,		DRER, Cpl.
Brown, Archibald	Norfolk	Clerk to Hartford
Brown, John	Norfolk	Shipbuilder, Merchant
Brown, spouse (John)	Norfolk	

NAME	RESIDENCE	VOCATION
Brown, child (John)	Norfolk	
Bruce, Robert	Norfolk	Clerk to Calderhead
Bryson, Peter	Norfolk	Clerk to Forsythe
Burton, Martin	Norfolk	Clerk
Butt, Patience[3]		
Byrd, William		DRER
Calderhead, William	Norfolk	Merchant/Lt. volunteers
Calderhead, children	Norfolk	
Calderhead, spouse	Norfolk	
Callaway, Archibald	Norfolk	Clerk to Farrar
Campbell, Archibald		
Campbell, Benjamin		DRER
Caryey, John Henry	Maryland	Master
Cayford, Richard	New Jersey	QOLV, off.
Clarkson, Basil	Eastern Shore	
Clayton, Joseph		DRER
Clegg, Richard	Norfolk	Clerk to Hargraves
Coakley, John	Norfolk	
Coakley, spouse (John)	Norfolk	
Coakley, William	Norfolk	
Coakley, William	Norfolk	Surgeon
Colbourne, Charles	Norfolk	
Collett, John		Merchant, QOLV
Cook, Jenny[1]		
Cooper, Robert		
Cornick, Africa		DRER
Cornicks, Roger		DRER
Cowan, Robert	Virginia	QOLV, off.
Crocus, John		DRER
Crouch,		DRER, Sgt.
Cunningham, Jonathan	Norfolk	Clerk to Gilmour
Cunningham, John	Norfolk	QOLV, officer
Cunningham, James	Norfolk	Clerk to Calderhead
Curl, Oliver		DRER

NAME	RESIDENCE	VOCATION
Curry, (sergeant)		DRER, Sgt.
Curry, (son of sgt.)		
Daily, James	Norfolk	Clerk to Gordon
Dale, Richard[4]		Officer, *Lady Susan*
Dameron, Jesse		DRER
Daniel, James		DRER
Dawson, James	Norfolk	Master
Dawson, Joyce	Norfolk	
Dawson, child	Norfolk	
Delany, Daniel		
Donaldson, William	Portsmouth	Storekeeper
Donaldson, spouse	Portsmouth	
Drew, Henry		DRER
Dunn, James	Norfolk	Volunteer
Dunn, James	Norfolk	
Dunn, child (James)	Norfolk	
Dunn, John	Norfolk	
Dunn, Joel	Norfolk	
Earle, Charles	Princess Anne	Surgeon
Earnshaw, John, Jr.		
Earnshaw, John, Sr.		
Eden, Sir Robert	Maryland	Governor
Edgar, Thomas	Norfolk	Master w/Shedden
Edwards, Belinda[1]		Eilbeck, John
Norfolk		
Eilbeck, Jonathan	Norfolk	Merchant
Eilbeck, spouse (Jonathan)	Norfolk	
Ellegood, Robert		DRER
Ellegood, Sampson		DRER
Essex, Thomas		DRER
Etheridge, Alice[1]		
Etheridge, John		DRER
Farer, Lancelot	Norfolk	
Farmer, Robert	Norfolk	Clerk to Jamieson
Farmer, Samuel	Norfolk	Merchant

NAME	RESIDENCE	VOCATION
Farmer, child (Samuel)	Norfolk	
Farmer, Susannah (Samuel)	Norfolk	
Farns, John	Portsmouth	Merchant
Farrer, Thomas	Norfolk	Merchant/Militia
Farrer, William[2]	Norfolk	Merchant
Farrer, spouse (Wm.)	Norfolk	
Farrer, child (Wm.)	Norfolk	
Fleming, Henry	Norfolk	Merchant, QOLV, Maj.
Flemming, Robert		DRER
Fleming, spouse (Rob.)	Norfolk	
Fleming, children (Rob.)	Norfolk	
Forsyth, William	Norfolk	Shoemaker
Frazer, Adam	Norfolk	
Frazer, Charles		DRER
Frazer, James	Norfolk	Shoemaker
Freeland, Alexander	Norfolk	Clerk to Brown
Fry, Samuel		DRER
Fryer, Stephen	York Co.	
Galbraith, Joseph		
Geohegan, Mr.	Somerset Co., MD	
Gilman, John		
Gilmour, John		
Gilmour, Robert	Norfolk	Merchant
Gimer, Samuel		DRER
Godwin, Peter		DRER
Goodrich, Bartlett	Norfolk	Master
Goodrich, Bridger	Norfolk	Master
Goodrich, John, Jr.	Norfolk	Master
Goodrich, John, Sr.	Norfolk	Merchant/Master
Goodrich, Margaret (John, Sr.)	Norfolk	
Goodrich, Richard	Norfolk	Master

NAME	RESIDENCE	VOCATION
Goodrich, children[2]	Norfolk	
Goodwin, Samuel		DRER
Goodrich, William		
Goodrich, spouse (Wm.)	Norfolk	
Gordon, Alexander	Norfolk	Physician
Gordon, Samuel		DRER
Grady, George		
Griffin, Charles		DRER
Griffin, Hanah[1]		
Grimes, Thomas		Major
Grymes, John Randolph	Middlesex Co.	QOLV, Capt.
Gallaspy, James	Norfolk	Clerk to Farmer
Glassford, James	Norfolk	Clerk to Jameison
Gilchrist, James	Norfolk	Clerk to Hansford
Hall, Thomas	Norfolk	Surgeon/QOLV, eng.
Hamilton, Phillis		Officer's servant
Hammond, Alexander	Norfolk	Clerk to Fleming
Hansford, Lewis	Norfolk	Merchant
Hansford, children	Norfolk	
Hansford, spouse	Norfolk	
Hardy, John	Norfolk	Merchant
Hardy, spouse	Norfolk	
Hardy, children	Norfolk	
Hargraves, William	Norfolk	Merchant
Hargraves, spouse	Norfolk	
Hargraves, children	Norfolk	
Harris, Joseph[2]	Hampton	Pilot
Harrison, Philip		DRER
Harwood, Calcott	Norfolk	Clerk to Eilbeck
Hatton, Walter	Accomac	Customs officer
Hawes, Jacob		DRER
Heath, Samuel		
Heferman, John	Portsmouth	Portmaster
Heiter, Hannah[1]		

NAME	RESIDENCE	VOCATION
Henderson, Jonathan	Norfolk	Clerk to Brown
Henly, Henry	Norfolk	Clerk to Forsythe
Hepburn, Thomas	Norfolk	Merchant
Herbert, Esther[1]		
Herbert, John Malcolm	Norfolk	Shipbuilder/Militia capt.
Hiell, John		
Hildreth, Isaac	Norfolk	House carpenter
Hodges, Josiah	Norfolk	Merchant
Hogwood, Daniel		DRER
Holsture, Moses		DRER
Hopkins, Grecian[1]		
Hopkins, Penelope[1]		
Horner, William		
Houston, Alexander	Virginia	Merchant/Militia
Hunter, John, Sr.	Portsmouth	Merchant
Hurt, Jenny[1]		
Ingram, James	Norfolk	Merchant/Prize commissioner
Ivy, China[1]		
Ivy, Jonas		DRER
Jack, Thomas		
Jackson, Edward[2]	Norfolk	Seaman
Jackson, Francis		DRER
Jameison, Neil	Norfolk	Merchant
Jameison, Samuel Heath	Accomac Co.	Merchant
Jennings, Thomas	Maryland	Ex. Atty. Gen'l of MD
Jolly, William		
Jones, Jasper		DRER
Jones, Owen		DRER
Jones, Philip		DRER
Keeling, Abel		DRER
Keeling, Jesse		DRER
Keeling, Jonathan Thorougood	Norfolk	Clerk to Fleming

NAME	RESIDENCE	VOCATION
Kellick, Elizabeth[1]		
Kennedy, William	Somerset Co., MD	QOLV
Kerr, John	Virginia	Clerk/Master
Kerr, Samuel	Norfolk	Merchant
King, Benjamin		DRER
King, John[2]		Seaman
Lawrence, Toby		DRER
Lawson, Joshua		DRER
Lecke, Sarah		Spouse of Lt. on *Roebuck*
Leyburn, Alexander	Maryland	Mariner
Leyburn, Peter	Eastern Shore	Merchant/Master
Leyburn, children	Eastern Shore	
Leyburn, spouse	Eastern Shore	
Lindsay, Samuel	Pennsylvania	QOLV, Lt./Suveyor
Logan, George	Princess Anne Co.	Merchant
Logan, children	Princess Anne Co.	
Logan, Isabella	Princess Anne Co.	Wife
Longwith, Benjamin		DRER
Lounds, John	Norfolk	Storekeeper
Love, Dilly[2]		
Love, Rachel[1]		
Lovett, Owen		DRER
Lyons, Charles	Princess Anne Co.	Planter
Lynch, Patrick	Norfolk	Clerk to Forsythe
MacAlister, Archibald	Norfolk	
MacAlister, Donald	Norfolk	
MacAlister, spouse (Donald)	Norfolk	
MacAlister, Hector	Norfolk	Master
MacDonald, Donald	Norfolk	Printer
Macki, Norfolk		DRER
Mackie, Richard	Nansemond Co.	Planter/Pilot
Mackie, Robert	Norfolk	Clerk to Gilmour
MacKnight, Mr.	Norfolk	
Maclean, John		
Mahoney, James		Seaman

Appendix

NAME	RESIDENCE	VOCATION
Maitland, William	Williamsburg	Merchant
Mallinson, Robert		
Martin, John Ponsonby	Virginia	
Mathews, Jeremiah	Norfolk	Clerk to Towse
McCall, Archibald	Norfolk	Clerk to Fleming
McCann, Andrew	Virginia	Queen's Ranger, Lt.
McCaw, Elizabeth	Virginia	
McCaw, James	Norfolk	Surgeon, apoth.
McCaw, children	Norfolk	
McCaw, spouse	Norfolk	
McClennan, Nelly		Officer's servant
McCulloch, Thomas	Norfolk	Merchant
McDowall, John	Virginia	Merchant
McKenny, William	Norfolk	Clerk to Fleming
McNeil, John		
McSween, Alexander	Norfolk	Clerk to McAlister
McTaggart, John	Norfolk	Merchant
Menzies, James	Williamsburg	Dunmore's Clerk
Miller, George[2]	Virginia	
Miller, Hugh	Norfolk	Merchant
Miller, James	Portsmouth	Merchant
Miller, Robert		
Mills, George[2]	Portsmouth	Seaman
Minze, Gabriel		DRER
Mirfield, Edward	Norfolk	Merchant
Mitchell, Bristol		DRER
Mitchell, Cary	Virginia	Collector-James
Mitchell, Mr.		Collector-Lower Dist. James River
Morgan, Willoughby	Norfolk	Master
Morgan, children	Norfolk	
Morgan, spouse	Norfolk	
Morris, Dinah[1]		
Morrison, Thomas		QOLV, ensign quartermaster
Moseley, Fanny[1]		

NAME	RESIDENCE	VOCATION
Moseley, Rose[1]		
Muir, George	Norfolk	Merchant
Muirhead, John	Norfolk	Shoemaker, mstr. privateer
Muirhead, children	Norfolk	
Muirhead, spouse	Norfolk	
Murray, James	Norfolk	Merchant, QOLV
Murray, John, Lord Dunmore		Governor
Nestor, Richard	Norfolk	Clerk to Goodrich
Newton, Frank		DRER
Nicholas, George		Comptroller-Upper Dist. James River
Nimmo, Abby[1]		
Nimmo, Davie		DRER
Nimmo, Moody		DRER
Nimmo, Susan[1]		
Norton, Mary Beth		
Ogilvie, James		
O'Hara, Cain	Norfolk	Tavernkeeper
Orange, William	Norfolk	
Paden, Lewis		DRER
Parker, Hannah[1]		
Parker, Navin		DRER
Parker, Thomas Hall		
Parker, Tony		DRER
Parker, William	Williamsburg	
Parker, children		
Parker, spouse		
Patient, John		
Payne, Nicholas	Williamsburg	Clerk to Hansford
Peeding, Mingo		DRER
Pew, John	Norfolk	Merchant/Militia
Phillips, Josiah	Princess Anne Co.	QOLV, off.
Pitt, Richard Floyd	Williamsburg	Upholsterer
Pitt, father of Richard	Williamsburg	Magazine keeper

NAME	RESIDENCE	VOCATION
Portsmouth, Sampson		DRER
Rae, George	Norfolk	Merchant
Ramsay, David	Norfolk	Seaman
Rand, Thomas		DRER
Redman, Isaac	Hampton	Pilot
Reed, James		DRER
Richardson, Joseph		
Riddell, George	Yorktown	Surgeon
Riddell, Susannah	Yorktown	
Roberts, Humphrey	Portsmouth	Merchant
Roberts, children	Portsmouth	
Roberts, spouse	Portsmouth	
Robertson, Charles	Norfolk	Merchant/Spy
Robinson, Abby[1]		
Robinson, Lucy[1]		
Robinson, Neal		DRER
Robinson, Pleasant[1]		
Robinson, Solomon		DRER
Robinson, Thomas		
Ross, Alexander	Norfolk	Merchant
Roxburgh, Anthony	Virginia	Merchant/Volun.
Royal, John P.		DRER, Corporal
Sands, Joseph	Virginia	Recruiter
Saunders, John	Princess Anne Co.	Planter/QOLV, Capt.
Saunders, children	Princess Anne Co.	
Saunders, spouse	Princess Anne Co.	
Savage, James		DRER
Savage, Susanna[1]		
Sawyer, Argyle		DRER
Schaw, John	Virginia	Commissary agent
Scott, Peter	Norfolk	Clerk to Hepburn
Scott, Robert		DRER
Shank, David	Virginia	QOLV, off.
Shedden, Robert	Portsmouth	Merchant
Sherlock, John	Accomac Co.	
Simonds, Joseph		

NAME	RESIDENCE	VOCATION
Simpson, Joseph		
Slater, Thomas		
Sparrow, Fanny		Servant, J. Ingram
Sprowl, Andrew	Portsmouth	Ship owner, Master, Merchant
Sprowl, Catherine	Portsmouth	
Stephens, John	Northampton Co.	Master
Stephens, children (John)	Northampton Co.	
Stephens, spouse (John)	Northampton Co.	
Stephens, Moses[2]	Virginia	Seaman
Stevens, John		DRER
Stewart, Robert	Portsmouth	Merchant
Stewart, Roger	Portsmouth	Merchant
Stewart, Thomas	Portsmouth	Blacksmith
Stuart, Caesar		DRER
Talbert, Andrew	Norfolk	Clerk to Hardy
Talbot, John		DRER
Taylor, Mary[1]		
Taylor, Robert	Norfolk	Clerk to Hansford
Thompson, Grace[1]		
Thompson, Jane	Norfolk	
Thompson, Talbot	Norfolk	Sailmaker
Thorougood, Thomas S.	Norfolk	Clerk to Gilmour
Throwgood, Francis		DRER
Throwgood, George		DRER
Throwgood, Kate[1]		
Throwgood, Peter		DRER
Throwgood, Phillis, Jr.		DRER
Throwgood, Phillis, Sr.		DRER
Throwgood, Scipio		DRER
Tinnible, Sepper		DRER
Towse, Francis	Norfolk	Blacksmith

NAME	RESIDENCE	VOCATION
Tucker, George		DRER
Tucker, Joseph		DRER
Tucker, Mathew[2]	Norfolk	Seaman
Tucker, Robert		DRER
Tucker, Thomas	Virginia	Militia
Veal, Sarah[1]		
Vessey, Joseph	Norfolk	Clerk to Calderhead
Vessey, William	Norfolk	Clerk to Calderhead
Villeroy, Maxmillian		DRER
Walker, Alexander		
Walker, John	Norfolk	Merchant
Walker, William	Portsmouth	Merchant
Wallace, Michael	Nansemond Co.	Merchant
Wallace, Michael		DRER
Wallace, Robert		DRER
Warden, Hugh	Virginia	Volunteer
Warwick, Alexander		
Warwick, Anthony	Nansemond Co.	Merchant
Watson, Jonathan	Gloucester Co.	
Wayland, Joseph	Maryland	Master, Pilot, Privateer
Weeks, Chrestia[2]	Norfolk	
Weeks, spouse[2]	Norfolk	Laborer/Brit. Army
Weeks, son[2]	Norfolk	Royal Service
Wells, Lewis		DRER
Wenright, George	Norfolk	Clerk to Farrar
White, James	Princess Anne Co.	Merchant
White, Thomas		DRER
Whitehurst, Nathaniel	Norfolk	Clerk to Farrar
Whitler, Annaki		DRER
Wilkie, John	Gloucester Co.	Pilot, Master
Williams, Elizabeth[1]		
Williams, Hannah[1]		
Williams, Mary[1]		
Williamson, Joseph		
Willoughby, Abby[1]		
Willoughby, Arculls		DRER

NAME	RESIDENCE	VOCATION
Willoughby, Dinah[1]		
Willoughby, Elizabeth[1]		
Willoughby, Esther[1]		
Willoughby, Esther[1]		
Willoughby, Glasgow		DRER
Willoughby, Jenny[1]		
Willoughby, Judith[1]		
Willoughby, Kate[1]		
Willoughby, Lettice[1]		
Willoughby, Manda[1]		
Willoughby, Mary[1]		
Willoughby, Peter		DRER
Willoughby, Robert		DRER
Wilson, Thomas	Norfolk	Clerk to Eilbeck
Woodhouse, George		DRER
Woodhouse, Maxmillian		DRER
Woodhouse, Owen		DRER
Wormington, John	Virginia	Dunmore's Custom Official
Wylie, Robert	Gloucester Co.	Merchant, Mariner
(no last name known):		
Billy		Postillion, Landon Carter
Chloe		Servant, J. McCaw
Glasgow		Servant, J. Ingram
Harry		Servant, J. Herbert
James		Servant, J. Herbert
Joe		Servant, L. Carter
John		Servant, L. Carter
Lancaster Sam		Servant, L. Carter
Manuel		Servant, L. Carter
Michael		DRER
Moses		Servant, L. Carter
Panticoke		Servant, L. Carter

NAME	RESIDENCE	VOCATION
Peter		Servant, L. Carter
Peter		Servant, Samuel Kerr
Phillis		Servant, Mrs. Bruff
Sam		Child of Chloe
Tom		Servant, L. Carter

DRER: Dunmore's Royal Ethiopian Regiment
QOLV: Queen's Own Loyal Virginian Regiment
[1] Spouse of members of Dunmore's Royal Ethiopians
[2] Free African American
[3] Children of member of Royal Ethiopians
[4] Dale was captured in 1776 and became an officer in the Continental Navy, eventually serving as first lieutenant under John Paul Jones.

Appendix 3

Patriots in the Gwynn's Island Campaign, May-August 1776

NAME	RESIDENCE	VOCATION
Anderson, John	Gloucester	
Anderson, Obadiah		
Armando, Ambrose		Naval forces
Armistead, Thomas		Naval forces
Arundel, Dohicky	(French)	VA military, Capt.
Ballentine, Church		Naval forces
Barryman, John		VA military
Bennett, Walker, Dr.		VA military, Surgeon
Billups, John	Gloucester/ Kingston	VA military, Lt.
Billups, Richard	Gloucester/ Kingston	Capt.
Bingham, Hugh		Naval forces
Blaws, James		Naval forces
Blaws, Robert		Naval forces
Bosworth, Obadiah	Gloucester	
Boucher, John Thomas		Naval forces/Capt.
Bramley, Philip	Gloucester	Naval forces
Branford, John		Naval forces
Bromley, Philip	Gloucester	
Bright, Francis		Naval forces

NAME	RESIDENCE	VOCATION
Brooke, Walter		Naval forces
Brown, Francis	Gloucester	Naval forces
Brown, Francis	Gloucester/ Kingston	VA military
Brown, William	Gloucester	
Buckner, William		Naval forces
Buckner, William		VA military, Col.
Butler, Edward		Pilot
Cabell, Nicholas		VA military, Capt.
Cabell, Samuel Jordan		VA military, 1st Lt.
Callender, Eleazer		Naval forces
Chaldron, Francis		Naval forces
Chapin, Benjamin		Naval forces/Surgeon
Clark, John		
Cocke, John Catesby		Naval & VA military forces
Collier, Thomas		VA military, Capt.
Cook, Robert		Naval forces
Cooper, Edward		Pilot
Crump, Abner		Naval forces
Culley, Robert		Naval forces
Dabney, Isaac		VA military, Col.
David, John		Naval forces
Daingerfield, William		VA military, Col.
Denny, Samuel		VA military, Capt.
Diggs, Simon	Gloucester/ Kingston	Shipbuilder
Dishman, James		
Dishman, John		
Dishman, William		
Donohow (Donohue), Henry		
Dunford, William		
Elam, Robert		Naval forces
Elliott, Jeduthan		Naval forces

NAME	RESIDENCE	VOCATION
Fog, William		VA military, Adj.
Foster, John, Jr.	Gloucester/ Kingston	VA military, Lt.
Foster, Peter	Gloucester/ Kingston	
Garland, Samuel		VA military, Capt.
Glenn, John		VA military, Maj.
Grayson, William		VA military, Col.
Hall, Robert	Gloucester	Naval forces
Hanway, Samuel		VA military
Harris, John		Naval forces
Harrison, Benj.		VA military, Col.
Harrison, Charles		VA military, Capt.
Herbert, Argyle		Naval forces
Hobday, Francis	Gloucester	Pilot
Horn (Hern), Francis	Gloucester/ Kingston	
Howe, Bannister	Gloucester	
Howe, Bannister	Gloucester	Naval forces
Hubbard, John		Naval forces
Hudgins, Anthony	Gloucester/ Kingston	VA military, Pvt.
Hudgins, Holder	Gloucester/ Kingston	VA military, Lt.
Hughes, Gabriel	Gloucester/ Kingston	VA military, Pvt.
James, Thomas	Gloucester/ Kingston	VA military
Jones, Robert	Gloucester	
Key, George		VA military, Pvt.
Lawson, John		VA military
Lee, John		Naval forces
Lee, William	Gloucester/ Kingston	Naval forces
Lewis, Charles		VA military, Col.

NAME	RESIDENCE	VOCATION
Lilly, Thomas	Gloucester/ Kingston	Naval forces
Lucas, Charles		Naval forces
Lucas, James		Naval forces
Markham, James		Naval forces
Masterson (Marsden), Thomas		Naval forces
McClanahan, William		VA military, Lt. Col.
Mitchell, Richard	Gloucester	
Mitchell, William		Naval forces
Moore, Edward		Naval forces
Moore, John		Naval forces
Moss, Francis		Naval forces
Moughon, George	Gloucester/ Kingston	
Murray, David		Naval forces
Nelson, William		VA military, Maj.
Page, John	Gloucester	Planter
Parsons, John	Gloucester	Shipbuilder
Partridge, Samuel	Gloucester	
Patterson, John		Naval forces
Penn, Abraham		VA military, Capt.
Peyton, Sir John	Gloucester	VA military, Co. Lt.
Pollard, Benjamin		Naval forces
Quarles, James		Naval forces
Quarles, John		VA military
Rakestraw, Robert		VA military, Adj.
Randall, Benjamin		Naval forces
Ransome, Augustine	Gloucester	
Ransome, Thomas	Gloucester	Naval forces
Read, Francis	Gloucester/ Kingston	
Richards, William		VA military
Richeson, Holt		VA military, Capt.
Rogers, Peter		VA military, Capt.

NAME	RESIDENCE	VOCATION
Rose, Alexander		VA military, 1st Lt.
Sadler, Robert		2nd VA Regiment
Singleton, Joshua	Gloucester	
Smith, Gregory		VA military, Capt.
Smith, William		VA military, Capt.
Stadler, John		Engineer
Stephen, Adam		VA military, Col.
Stephens, Richard		VA military
Stuffs, John	Gloucester/ Kingston	
Taliaferro, Benjamin		VA military, 2nd Lt.
Taliaferro, Philip		VA military
Taliaferro, William		VA military
Taylor, Francis		VA military, Col.
Taylor, John		VA military
Throckmorton, Mordecai		VA military
Tompkies, Charles		VA military
Tompkins, Christopher		Naval forces
Tompkins, Robert		
Tool, Richard		Naval forces
Triplett, George		Naval forces
Triplett, Reuben		Naval forces
Turner, James		VA military, Capt.
Umphries, James		Naval forces
Valentine, Jacob		Naval forces
Weedon, George		VA military, Col.
Weston, Diggs		VA military
Wilkinson, Stephen		Naval forces
Williams, William		Naval and VA military forces
Wright, Patrick		Naval forces
Yeatman, Thomas	Gloucester/ Kingston	VA military, Lt.

Appendix 4

Military Units in the Gwynn's Island Campaign

BRITISH

14th Regiment
Queen's Own Loyal Virginia Regiment (Loyalist)
(Lord) Dunmore's Royal Ethiopian Regiment (Loyalist)
Royal Marines (from HMS *Roebuck, Fowey, Otter*)
Royal Navy Sailors

AMERICAN (Patriot)

1st Virginia Regiment of Foot
2nd Virginia Regiment of Foot
3rd Virginia Regiment of Foot
4th Virginia Regiment of Foot
5th Virginia Regiment of Foot
6th Virginia Regiment of Foot
7th Virginia Regiment of Foot
8th Virginia Regiment of Foot
9th Virginia Regiment of Foot
Virginia Artillery Company, 1776
2nd Battalion of Minutemen, 1776
Lancaster District Battalion

Notes

Chapter 1

1. The Declaration of Independence, printed by John Dunlap in 1777, Philadelphia. House, *The Declaration of Independence and the Constitution*, 96th Cong., 1st sess., 1979, House Doc. 96-143, 3.

2. Loyalist efforts are best developed in Adele Hast's *Loyalism in Revolutionary Virginia, The Norfolk Area and the Eastern Shore*, published by the Studies in America History and Culture, ed. Robert Berkhofer, no. 34 (Ann Arbor: UMI Research Press, 1983). William Leo Moran's "The Origins of the British Expedition to the Carolinas, 1775-1776" (M.A. Thesis, The College of William and Mary, 1966) provides a broader perspective on loyalists in this time.

3. The term "floating town" was coined by Captain Andrew S. Hamond, who served as Commodore of the Royal Navy forces supporting Governor Dunmore between February and August, 1776.

4. The best and most thorough study of Dunmore remains Percy B. Caley's "Dunmore: Colonial Governor of New York and Virginia, 1770-1782" (Ph.D. dissertation, University of Pittsburgh, 1939).

5. Patricia Givens Johnson, *General Andrew Lewis of Roanoke and Greenbrier* (Blacksburg, VA: by the author, Southern Printing Co., Inc., 1973), 87-92.

6. News of Lexington and Concord followed soon after the gunpowder incident. The similarity of the actions by both Governor Dunmore and General Gage hinted at a British conspiracy.

7. The presence of Dunmore's family, aides, and servants in Williamsburg's poorly garrisoned and fortified Governor's Palace strongly influenced his relocation to Yorktown.

8. Hast, 46-9.

9. Moran, 2-4.

10. United States Navy Department, *Naval Documents of the American Revolution* (hereafter cited as NDAR), vol. 2, ed. William Bell Clark (Washington, D.C.: U.S. Government Printing Office, 1966), 66, 74, 100, 101, 111, 113, 122, 123, 125. Following a hurricane, vessels from the floating town were driven ashore. This began a series of direct confrontations with residents and escalated into larger incidents.

11. NDAR, Vol. 3, 511, 529, 545, 565, 574, 575. Dunmore seized the printing press on September 30. The Kemp's Landing skirmish occurred on October 18. Minor raids by Dunmore followed.

12. NDAR, vol. 2, 920-22, 1052-54, 1062. The emancipation document was prepared by Dunmore aboard his flagship *William* on November 7 and issued one week later following the successful rout of militia near Great Bridge.

13. NDAR, vol. 3, 25-29, 39, 40, 74-75, 78-79.

14. NDAR, vol. 3, 579, 592, 617-21, 661, 704, 1187.

15. In 1777 Norfolk officials convened a committee to assess the damage. Their figures fixed responsibility for destruction of property by each side.

16. Hopkins' delay in fitting out the American fleet and the arrival of the *Roebuck* prevented an early confrontation with Dunmore.

17. Hamond's early association with Dunmore is covered well by William Hugh Moomaw's "The Naval Career of Captain Hamond, 1775-79" (unpublished Ph.D. dissertation, University of Virginia, 1955), 26-27, 33-34.

18. Percy B. Caley, "Dunmore: Colonial Governor of New York and Virginia, 1770-1782" (unpublished Ph.D. dissertation, University of Pittsburgh, 1939), 781-82.

19. NDAR, vol. 3, 1349-50; vol. 4, 55, 101-2.

20. Clinton was unimpressed with Dunmore's efforts and upon arriving at Wilmington was convinced his troopships could not successfully negotiate the Cape Fear River.

21. NDAR, vol. 4, 1298-99; Caley, 788-92.

22. Caley, 802-5.

Chapter 2

1. The relationship of the Powhatans and some of their best-known

representatives—Powhatan, Opecancanough, and Pocahontas—are being closely examined and revised. Their interconnection to the Jamestown colonists is well documented. Their role in the support of individual colonists, such as Hugh Gwynn, may be developed someday with more substance than is currently available.

2. Nell Marion Nugent, ed., *Cavaliers and Pioneers, Abstracts of Virginia Land Patents and Grants 1623-1666*, vol. 2 (Baltimore: Genealogical Publishing Company, 1969), 132, 141, 182, 239, 243, 247-48, 263, 265.

3. Nugent, 141, 290.

4. Mathews County Memorial Library, Mathews, Virginia, Vertical File, Gwynn.

5. Gwynn prospered in a growing colony. Immigration from England brought many to the colonies as a result of the English Civil War. Trade remained unregulated until the reign of Oliver Cromwell.

6. John W. Reps, *Tidewater Towns* (Williamsburg: University of Virginia Press, 1972), 65-67, 78.

7. Reps, 142-43.

8. The 1704 Virginia Quit Rent Rolls show Capt. Gwynn, 1,100 acres; Benjamin Read, 550 acres; and Walter Keeble, 550 acres.

9. The Virginia Colonial Records Project (hereinafter cited as the VCRP) contains selected British records and is located in the Colonial Williamsburg Foundation Library in Williamsburg, Virginia. The number given represents the abstracted document. Full documents are referenced through the abstracts with an "M" number (microfilm). This incident is VCRP 4185.

10. Sister June Meredith Costin, S.S.N.D., "Shipping in Yorktown, Virginia 1740-1744 (unpublished Ph.D. dissertation, College of William and Mary in Virginia, 1973).

11. VCRP 5607. The *Betty and Jenny* appears in both Virginia and Barbadian records.

12. Gloucester County Surveyors Book "A," 1733-1810, p. 33, filed by John Throckmorton, 13 December 1754 for Thomas and Jonathan Brooks. Gloucester County Court House, Virginia.

13. A list of Gwynn vessels was compiled by the author from both the VCRP and the records of "entrances and clearances" for the six colonial Virginia ports. These vessels span the years 1743 to 1788, and were owned and/or captained by John, Walter, Hugh, William, and George Gwynn. They include the *Ruby, Betty and Jenny, Friendship, James, Endeavor, Baltimore Packet, Whim, Cato, Amity*, and *Fanny*.

14. Gwynn preferences in sailing rigs correspond to findings by Costin (n. 10).

15. Over half of known Gwynn vessels were schooners.

16. Peter Jennings Wrike, "Mathews County Shipbuilding Patterns 1780-1860" (unpublished M.A. thesis, Old Dominion University, 1990), 48-49, 111.

17. David M. Ludlum, *Early American Hurricanes, 1492-1870, The History of American-Weather* (Boston: American Meteorological Society, 1966), 23-27.

18. *Virginia Gazette*, Purdie and Dixon, Sept.-Oct., 1769.

19. Emma R. Matheny and Helen K. Yates, eds., *Kingston Parish Register, Gloucester and Mathews Counties 1754-1827* (Richmond: by the editors, 1963), 117.

20. Robert L. Scribner and Brent Tartar, eds., *Revolutionary Virginia: The Road to Independence*, vol. 2 (Charlottesville: University of Virginia, 1975), 163-64.

21. "Virginia Legislative Papers: The Case of John Wilkie of Gloucester," *Virginia Magazine of History and Biography* 15 (1908): 292-95.

22. H. R. McIlwaine, *Legislative Journals of the Council of Colonial Virginia*, vol. 3 (Richmond: Virginia State Library, 1919), 506.

Chapter 3

1. William Hugh Moomaw, "The Naval Career of Captain Hamond, 1775-79" (unpublished Ph.D. dissertation, University of Virginia, 1955), 187-88. Courtesy on board British warships was ritual.

2. *Naval Documents of the American Revolution* (hereafter cited as NDAR), vol. 5, ed. William Bell Clark (Washington, D.C.: U.S. Government Printing Office, 1966), 174, 321.

3. NDAR, vol. 5, 321; Percy B. Caley, "Dunmore: Colonial Governor of New York and Virginia, 1770-1782" (unpublished Ph.D. dissertation, University of Pittsburgh, 1939), 802-5.

4. Edward A. Smyth, "Mob Violence in Prerevolutionary Norfolk, Virginia" (unpublished M.A. Thesis, Old Dominion University, 1965).

5. Moomaw, 192-93.

6. NDAR, vol. 5, 321; Moomaw, 193. The destination for the floating town could not have been firmly determined. Water and supplies as well as embarkation of all personnel had to be completed. At that time an accurate assessment of destination was possible. Gwynn's Island was a strong possibility, but whether it was a temporary destination or a permanent one is not clear.

7. NDAR, vol. 5, 222, 223, 234.

8. NDAR, vol. 5, 240, 258.

9. NDAR, vol. 5, 258-59.

10. See note 6. Hamond and Dunmore had worked together for three days on a common purpose. Now that their resources were known and a tenuous working relationship established full cooperation, and agreement on a destination was possible.

11. NDAR, vol. 5, 321.

12. NDAR, vol. 5, 235-36, 256, 278.

13. NDAR, vol. 5, 288-89, 321; Moomaw, 204-5.

14. NDAR, vol. 5, 278. The sailing route is traditional and the navigational hazards the same then as now. The *Roebuck* maintained station off Windmill Point for virtually all their stay at Gwynn's Island.

15. Moomaw, 194.

16. Moomaw, 194-95.

Chapter 4

1. William Hugh Moomaw, "The Naval Career of Captain Hamond, 1775-79" (unpublished Ph.D. dissertation, University of Virginia, 1955), 194. The size of the invasion force was best described by William Barry, a prisoner aboard the *Roebuck*, in *Naval Documents of the American Revolution* (hereafter cited as NDAR), vol. 5, ed. William Bell Clark (Washington, D.C.: U.S. Government Printing Office, 1966), 483-85. The method of attack is traditional and follows the terrain encountered. The island has suffered much erosion since 1776 but can be reconstructed from topographical surveys shown on sheet 2 of the Chesapeake Bay Map, published in 1863. Copies of the prepublication data and the published chart are in the U.S. National Archives Cartographic Division in Alexandria, Virginia.

2. See note 1. Moomaw, 195-96; Percy B. Caley, "Dunmore: Colonial Governor of New York and Virginia, 1770-1782" (unpublished Ph.D. dissertation, University of Pittsburgh, 1939), 813-14.

3. Caley, 814; NDAR, vol. 5, 840.

4. Moomaw, 206; "Dunmore's Well" is noted on deeds of Mathews County (old Kingston Parish—Gloucester County) as late as 1821. Survey by Isaac Foster, 18 September 1821 of 290 acres on Gwynn's Island. "Beginning at 1 (a) corner on the Piankatank Shore near Dunmores Well. . . .," Survey book, Matthews County 1811-1840. Copy in Virginia State Archives, Richmond, Virginia. By 1933 the location of the well, known to living residents, had eroded along with the shoreline.

5. The locations, cited previously, are shown on Figure 7.

6. Moomaw, 195; NDAR, vol. 5, 460.

7. NDAR, vol. 5, 665-69.

8. See note 7. This fine account reveals the inability to maintain security in the floating town and the ease of escape.

9. NDAR, vol. 5, 288-89, 301.

10. The diary of Miguel Antonio Eduardo is in NDAR, vol. 5, Appendix B, 1139-51.

11. NDAR, vol. 5, 1341-42.

12. NDAR, vol. 5, 310-11.

13. NDAR, vol. 5, 311-12.

14. It was unusual that Andrew Sprowl's death received no notice from either Dunmore or Hamond. Since before June 1775, Sprowl was one of the most powerful figures in Virginia. Sprowl's grave on Gwynn's Island, noted by the patriots, was larger than others around it.

15. NDAR, vol. 5, 1342.

16. NDAR, vol. 5, 1343.

17. NDAR, vol. 5, 342-43.

18. Moomaw, 216-17.

19. NDAR, vol. 5, 1343.

20. NDAR, vol. 5, 1344.

21. NDAR, vol. 5, 364.

22. NDAR, vol. 5, 669. This account of John Emmes is similar in circumstances to that of William Barry.

23. NDAR, vol. 5, 840. The creation of a ditch and embankment to protect Dunmore's troops duplicates his efforts earlier at Portsmouth.

24. NDAR, vol. 5, 669, 500.

25. Benjamin Quarles' "Lord Dunmore as Liberator," *William and Mary Quarterly*, 3rd series, 11 (1958): 494-507, discusses the "numbers" issue very astutely.

26. NDAR, vol. 5, 463.

27. NDAR, vol. 5, 460-61.

28. NDAR, vol. 5, 460-61.

29. NDAR, vol. 5, 500.

30. NDAR, vol. 5, 1345.

31. Since the capture of the *Santa Barbara* was a naval affair, Hamond dealt principally with the Spanish. Eduardo's account, over time reveals some of both Hamond's and Dunmore's personalities. His dates for events sometimes are incorrect but he clearly remembers conversations and the tone of meetings.

32. NDAR, vol. 5, 535-36.

33. NDAR, vol. 5, 569-71.

34. NDAR, vol. 5, 1345.

Chapter 5

1. The events of Catherine Sprowl's odyssey are reconstructed from her petition in *Naval Documents of the American Revolution* (hereafter cited as NDAR), vol. 5, ed. William Bell Clark (Washington, D.C.: U.S. Government Printing Office, 1966), 776-77.

2. Catherine Hunger Sprowl had only recently married Andrew. As Catherine Hunter she had exasperated Dunmore in the fall of 1775 with demands. The Hunters and Sprowls represented two powerful Tidewater mercantile families used to a standard of living not dissimilar to the Governor.

3. NDAR, vol. 5, 685.

4. NDAR, vol. 5, 670-71, 686, 687-88.

5. NDAR, vol. 5, 776-77.

6. NDAR, vol. 5, 1345.

7. Ibid.; William Hugh Moomaw, "The Naval Career of Captain Hamond, 1775-1779" (unpublished Ph.D. dissertation, University of Virginia, 1955), 224-25.

8. NDAR, vol. 5, 1345.

9. Moomaw, 225-26.

10. Moomaw, 224; NDAR, vol. 5, 1345.

11. NDAR, vol. 5, 743, 755-56.

12. According to Barbadian Clearance Records (Colonial Williamsburg Library, Microfilm M-223), Walsh only shipped two cargos in 1776. NDAR, vol. 5, 755.

13. Moomaw, 224-25.

14. NDAR, vol. 5, 757.

15. NDAR, vol. 5, 756-58.

16. NDAR, vol. 5, 757.

17. NDAR, vol. 5, 776-77.

18. NDAR, vol. 5, 793-94.

19. As suggested in note 2, an enmity between Sprowl, his widow, and their long-standing stature in the community may account for the otherwise inexplicable action by Dunmore.

Chapter 6

1. William Hugh Moomaw, "The Naval Career of Captain Hamond, 1775-1779" (unpublished Ph.D. dissertation, University of Virginia, 1955), 227-32.

2. *Naval Documents of the American Revolution* (hereafter cited as NDAR), vol. 5, ed. William James Morgan (Washington, D.C.: U.S. Government Printing Office, 1970), 569-71, 716-17.

3. NDAR, vol. 5, 569-71, 740-41.

4. NDAR, vol. 5, 740-41.

5. NDAR, vol. 5, 754-55, 775, 820; Moomaw, 227-28.

6. Moomaw, 231.

7. Moomaw, 233-34.

8. NDAR, vol. 5, 862.

9. Percy B. Caley, "Dunmore: Colonial Governor of New York and Virginia, 1770-1782" (unpublished Ph.D. dissertation, University of Pittsburgh, 1939), 818-19; NDAR, vol. 5, 939.

10. Lewis's intelligence of British strength was limited to observation and deserter reports. With that information Dunmore would appear to be in a defensive posture. However, with Clinton's force still unaccounted for the possibility of overwhelming British reinforcement loomed.

11. Clinton's visit to Dunmore in February 1776 was well known. His return was a possibility.

12. General Lewis knew that news of a declaration of independence might bring retaliation from Dunmore and/or other British forces. As military commander of Virginia the initiative for action, once independence was declared, was his.

13. The absence and preoccupation of Virginia's leadership in this period allowed General Lewis great latitude in his choice of actions.

14. Moomaw, 233.

15. Moomaw, 232-33.

16. Patricia Givens Johnson, *General Andrew Lewis of Roanoke and Greenbrier* (Blacksburg, VA: by the author, Southern Printing Co., Inc., 1973), 205; NDAR, vol. 5, 1022-23.

17. Moomaw, 234; NDAR, vol. 5, 996-97. Tide tables for July 2, 1776 through July 15, 1776 were prepared in 1991 at the Virginia Institute of Marine Science at Gloucester Point, Virginia. The Institute is part of the College of William and Mary in Virginia. The tide tables were prepared by Arthur L. Edwards, using the VIMS-SMS Computer Center Tide Calendar. These results correlate to notations and events in the logs of the Royal Navy vessels *Roebuck*, *Otter*, and *Levant*.

18. Johnson, 205-6.

19. Moomaw, 235; NDAR, vol. 5, 1978-79, 1984; Percy B. Caley, "Dunmore: Colonial Governor of New York and Virginia, 1770-1782" (unpublished Ph.D. dissertation, University of Pittsburgh, 1939), 832-33.

Notes to Chapter 7

1. Naval Documents of the American Revolution (hereafter cited as NDAR), vol. 5, ed. William James Morgan (Washington, D.C.: U.S. Government Printing Office, 1970), 1068-69, 1078-79, 1984, 1022-23.

2. Percy B. Caley, "Dunmore: Colonial Governor of New York and Virginia, 1770-1782" (unpublished Ph.D. dissertation, University of Pittsburgh, 1939), 833-34.

3. NDAR, 1068-69, 1078-79, 1094-95, 1022-23, 1149-50; Caley, 834-37; William Hugh Moomaw, "The Naval Career of Captain Hamond, 1775-79" (unpublished Ph.D. dissertation, University of Virginia, 1955), 236.

4. Computation of the total firing by the Americans is based on material in Adrian Caruana's *The Light 6-Pdr. Battalion Gun of 1776* (Bloomfield, Ont. Canada: Museum Restoration Service, 1977), 25-30.

5. NDAR, vol. 5, 1150-51.

6. Patricia Givens Johnson, *General Andrew Lewis of Roanoke and Greenbrier* (Blacksburg, VA: by the author, Southern Printing Co., Inc., 1973), 207; NDAR, vol. 5, 1094-95.

7. Moomaw, 236.

8. Moomaw, 237.

9. NDAR, vol. 5, 1094-95, 1149-50; Caley, 837-38.

10. NDAR, vol. 5, 1094-95; Caley, 837-38; Johnson, 207.

11. Caley, 839.

12. Caley, 840-41.

13. NDAR, vol. 5, 1150.

14. NDAR, vol. 5, 1023.

15. Caley, 841.

16. Caley, 841; NDAR, vol. 5, 1050, 1150.

17. Moomaw, 239; NDAR, vol. 5, 1346.

18. NDAR, vol. 5, 1030, 1066.

19. NDAR, vol. 5, 1050.

Notes to Chapter 8

1. Naval Documents of the American Revolution (hereafter cited as NDAR), vol. 5, ed. William James Morgan (Washington, D.C.: U.S. Government Printing Office, 1970), 1066.

2. NDAR, vol. 5, 1119, 1346-47.

3. NDAR, vol. 5, 1119; William Hugh Moomaw, "The Naval Career of Captain Hamond, 1775-79" (unpublished Ph.D. dissertation, University of Virginia, 1955), 240-41.

4. NDAR, vol. 5, 1119, 1106, 1146.

5. NDAR, vol. 5, 1135-38.

6. NDAR, vol. 5, 1138-39; Moomaw, 241-42.

7. Moomaw, 242-43; NDAR, vol. 5, 1163-64.

8. NDAR, vol. 5, 1183-84; Moomaw, 242-43.

9. NDAR, vol. 5, 1312-14, 1206-7, 1234.

10. NDAR, vol. 5, 1250, 1194.

11. NDAR, vol. 5, 1250-51. During this expedition Governor Eden wrote Daniel Wolstenholme, Collector of Customs for the North Potomac and a loyalist. Eden wanted to provide passage for Wolstenholme but the Maryland Convention forbade such action. NDAR, vol. 5, 1163, 1220.

12. NDAR, vol. 5, 1275-76, 1263.

13. NDAR, vol. 5, 1275, 1347; Moomaw, 243.

14. NDAR, vol. 5, 1275-76.

15. NDAR, vol. 5, 1263, 1275.

16. NDAR, vol. 5, 1314, 1347.

17. NDAR, vol. 5, 1348, 1297, 1316.

18. NDAR, vol. 6, 24, 26; Percy B. Caley, "Dunmore: Colonial Governor of New York and Virginia, 1770-1782" (unpublished Ph.D. dissertation, University of Pittsburgh, 1939), 860.

19. NDAR, vol. 5, 1312-14.

20. NDAR, vol. 6, 51, 66.

21. NDAR, vol. 6, 51.

22. NDAR, vol. 5, 1348; vol. 6, 65; Moomaw, 246-47.

23. NDAR, vol. 6, 66, 88-89.

24. NDAR, vol. 6, 66-69, 174; Moomaw, 248.

25. Moomaw, 250; NDAR, vol. 6, 142, 174.

26. Caley, 866.

Notes to Chapter 9

1. Naval Documents of the American Revolution (hereafter cited as NDAR), vol. 5, ed. William James Morgan (Washington, D.C.: U.S. Government Printing Office, 1970), 1349-51.

2. NDAR, vol. 5, 1146.

3. Robert K. Wright, Jr., *The Continental Army*, Army Lineage Series (Washington, D.C.: Center of Military History, United States Army, 1983), 283-89, 335-36.

4. E. M. Sanchez-Saavedra, *A Guide to Virginia Military Organizations in the American Revolution, 1774-1787* (Richmond: Virginia State Library, 1978), 91, 98, 139, 29, 39, 15, 38, 30, 47.

5. Sanchez-Saavedra, 185-86.

6. Sanchez-Saavedra, 186-87.

7. Edward C. Papenfuse et al., eds., *A Biographical Dictionary of the Maryland Legislature, 1635-1789*, vol. 1: A-H (Baltimore: The Johns Hopkins University Press, 1979), 299-300. Later Eden's remains were removed to St. Anne's Churchyard in Annapolis.

8. NDAR, vol. 6, 184; Caley, 872.

9. Caley, 872-76.

10. Caley, 877-80.

11. John E. Selby, *Dunmore*, ed. Edward M. Riley (Williamsburg: Virginia Independence Bicentennial Commission, 1977), 64-65.

12. Selby, 65-66.

13. Selby, 66-67.

14. Selby, 69-74.

15. Selby, 74-75.

16. William Hugh Moomaw, "The Naval Career of Captain Hamond, 1775-79" (unpublished Ph.D. dissertation, University of Virginia, 1955); Paul P. Hoffman, ed., *Guide to the Naval Papers of Sir Andrew Snape Hamond, bart., 1766-1783 and Sir Graham Eden Hamond, bart., 1799-1825* (Charlottesville: University of Virginia Library, 1966), 12.

17. Hoffman, 13, 20.

18. Hoffman, 13-14, 19-20, 21-22.

19. Mathews County Legislative Petitions, Virginia State Archives, Richmond, Virginia, 12 December 1798.

20. *Virginia Gazette*, Williamsburg, 6 September 1776.

21. Gloucester County Legislative Petitions, Virginia State Archives, Richmond, Virginia, 7 November 1776.

22. NDAR, vol. 6, 88, 366, 1242; Mathews County Memorial Library, Mathews, Virginia, Vertical File, Billups; Peter Jennings Wrike, "Mathews County Shipbuilding Patterns 1780-1860" (unpublished M.A. thesis, Old Dominion University, 1990), 23-24.

23. VCRP 5901, High Court of Admiralty Prize Papers, 1779, HCA 32/91 British Publish Records Office.

24. "Virginia Legislative Papers: The Case of John Wilkie of Gloucester," *Virginia Magazine of History and Biography* 15 (1908): 292-95.

25. Ernest M. Eller, ed., *The Chesapeake Bay in the American Revolution* (Centerville, MD: Tidewater Publishers, 1981), 393-4.

26. Eller, 389-91.

27. John E. Selby, *The Revolution in Virginia 1775-1783* (Williamsburg: The Colonial Williamsburg Foundation, 1988), 45-46, 307-09.

Bibliography

Primary Sources

Boyd, Julian P., ed. *The Papers of Thomas Jefferson.* 19 vols. to date. Princeton: Princeton University Press, 1950-.

Force, Peter, ed. *American Archives: Consisting of a Collection of Authentic Records, State Papers, Debates and Letters.* 4th Ser., 6 vols., 5th Ser., 3 vols. Washington, D.C.: M. St. Claire Walker and Peter Force, 1836-1853.

Ford, Worthington C., ed. *Journals of the Continental Congress, 1774-1789.* 34 vols. Washington, D.C. U.S. Government Printing Office, 1904-1937.

Hamond, A.S. Hamond Papers. Charlottesville: University of Virginia Library.

McIlwaine, H. R., ed. *Legislative Journals of the Council of Colonial Virginia.* 3 vols. Richmond: Virginia State Library, 1919.

Nugent, Nell Marion, ed. *Cavaliers and Pioneers, Abstracts of Virginia Land Patents and Grants 1623-1666,* vol. 1. Baltimore: Genealogical Publishing Company, 1969.

Richmond, Virginia. Virginia State Archives. Legislative Petitions. Mathews County.

Richmond, Virginia. Gloucester County.

―――. Public Service Claims. Gloucester County.

Scribner, Robert L. and Brent Tarter, eds. *Revolutionary Virginia: The Road to Independence*. 6 vols. Charlottesville: University of Virginia, 1973-1981.

U.S. Congress. House. 1979. *The Declaration of Independence and the Constitution*. 96th Congress, 1st session, House Doc. 96-143.

United States Navy Department. *Naval Documents of the American Revolution*. William Bell Clark, William James Morgan, and William S. Dudley, eds. 9 vols. to date. Washington, D.C.: United States Government Printing Office, 1964-.

Williamsburg, Virginia. College of William and Mary. Swem Library Manuscript Department. Gloucester County Papers.

―――. Colonial Williamsburg Foundation Library. Virginia Colonial Records Project. The Survey Reports. Bound photostats of originals and microfilm.

―――. John Page Papers.

Wingo, Elizabeth B. and Bruce W., comp. *Norfolk County Tithables 1766-1780*. Norfolk: Published by the compilers, 5916 Powhatan Avenue, Norfolk, Virginia 23508, 1985.

Secondary Sources

Anderson, D.R., ed. "The Letters of Col. William Woodford, Col. Robert Howe and Gen. Charles Lee to Edmund Pendleton." Richmond College Historical Papers 1 (1915): 96-163.

Burgess, Louis A., comp. *Virginia Soldiers of 1776: Compiled from Documents on File in the Virginia Land Office Together with Material Found in the Archives Department of the Virginia State Library, and Other Reliable Sources*. 3 vols. Richmond: Richmond Press, 1927-1929.

Caley, Percy B. "Dunmore: Colonial Governor of New York and Virginia, 1770-1782." Unpublished Ph.D. dissertation, University of Pittsburgh, 1939.

Campbell, Charles, ed. *The Orderly Book of That Portion of the American Army Stationed at or near Williamsburg, Virginia, Under the Command of General Andrew Lewis from March 18th 1776 to August 28 1776.* Richmond: privately printed, 1860.

Chamberlayne, C. J., ed. *The Vestry Book of Kingston Parish, Gloucester County, Virginia.* Richmond: Old Dominion Press, 1929.

Chyrsosomides, Mary. "The Effect of the Revolution on Norfolk Politics." Unpublished M.A. thesis, Old Dominion University, 1986.

Costin, Sister June Meredith, S.S.N.D. "Shipping in Yorktown, Virginia 1740-1744." Unpublished Ph.D. dissertation, College of William and Mary in Virginia, 1973.

Creecy, John Harvle, ed. *Virginia Antiquary I.* Richmond: The Dietz Press, Inc., 1954.

Curtis, George M., III. "The Goodrich Family and the Revolution in Virginia, 1774-1776." *Virginia Magazine of History and Biography* 84 (1976): 49-74.

D'Auberteuil, Hillard. "List of French Officers Who Served in the American Armies with Commissions from Congress Prior to the Treaties Made Between France and the Thirteen United States of America." *Magazine of American History* 3 (1879): 364-69.

Eckenrode, H.J. "List of the Revolutionary Soldiers of Virginia." *Special Report of the Department of Archives and History for 1911.* Richmond: Virginia State Library Board, 1912.

———. "List of the Revolutionary Soldiers of Virginia; Supplement." *Special Report of the Department of Archives and History for 1912.* Richmond: Virginia State Library Board, 1913.

Eller, Ernest M., ed. *Chesapeake Bay in the American Revolution.* Centerville, MD: Tidewater Publishers, 1981.

Gwathmey, John H. *Historical Register of Virginians in the Revolution: Soldiers, Sailors, Marines.* Richmond: Dietz Press, 1938.

Haarmann, Albert W. "American Provincial Corps Authorized by Lord Dunmore, 1775." *Journal of the Society for Army Historical Research* 52

(1974): 254-55.

Harrison, Fairfax. "The Goodriches of Isle of Wight County, Virginia." *Tyler's Quarterly Historical and Genealogical Magazine* 2 (1920): 130-31.

Hast, Adele. *Loyalism in Revolutionary Virginia, the Norfolk Area and the Eastern Shore*. Published by the Studies in American History and Culture, no. 34. Ann Arbor: UMI Research Press, 1983.

Henderson, Patrick. "Smallpox and Patriotism: The Norfolk Riots 1768-1769." *Virginia Magazine of History and Biography* 73 (1965): 413-24.

Hoffman, Paul P., ed. *Guide to the Naval Papers of Sir Andrew Snape Hamond, bart., 1766-1783 and Sir Graham Eden Hamond, bart., 1799-1825*. Charlottesville: University of Virginia Library, 1966.

Johnson, Patricia Givens. *General Andrew Lewis of Roanoke and Greenbrier*. Blacksburg, VA: by the author, Southern Printing Co., Inc., 1973.

Lewis, Elizabeth Dutton, comp. *Revolutionary War Roster*. Gloucester, VA: published by the author, n.d.

The Lower Norfolk County Virginia Antiquary 1-5 (1895-1904). Reprint (5 vols. in 2) New York: Peter Smith, 1951.

Ludlum, David M. *Early American Hurricanes 1492-1870. The History of American Weather*. Boston: American Meteorological Society, 1966.

Luykx, John M. "Fighting for Food: British Foraging Operations at St. George's Island." *Maryland Historical Magazine* 71 (1976): 212-19.

Martin, Joseph. *A New and Comprehensive Gazetteer of Virginia and the District of Columbia*. Charlottesville, VA: by the author, 1835.

Mason, Frances Norton, ed. *John Norton & Sons, Merchants of London and Virginia*. Richmond: Dietz Press, 1937.

Mason, Polly Cary, ed. *Records of Colonial Gloucester County, Virginia*. 2 vols. Ann Arbor, MI: Edwards Bros., 1946-1948.

Matheny, Emma R., and Helen K. Yates, ed. *Kingston Parish Register, Gloucester and Mathews Counties 1754-1827*. Richmond, VA: by the editors, 1963.

Mathews, Virginia. Mathews County Memorial Library, Vertical File, Billups, Gwynn.

Moomaw, William Hugh. "The Naval Career of Captain Hamond, 1775-1779." Unpublished Ph.D. dissertation, University of Virginia, 1955.

Moran, William Leo. "The Origins of the British Expedition to the Carolinas 1775-1776." Unpublished M.A. thesis, College of William and Mary, 1966.

Morgan, William James. "The Governor's Floating Town." *The Iron Worker* (Autumn 1972): 1-9.

Naisawald, Louis Van Loan. "Robert Howe's Operations in Virginia, 1775-1776." *Virginia Magazine of History and Biography* 60 (1952): 437-43.

Noël Hume, Ivor. *1775: Another Part of the Field*. New York: Alfred A. Knopf, 1966.

Palmer, Gregory. *Biographical Sketches of Loyalists of the American Revolution*. Westport, CT: Meckler Publishing, 1984.

Papenfuse, Edward C., Alan F. Day, David W. Jordan, and Gregory A. Stiverson, eds. *A Biographical Dictionary of the Maryland Legislature, 1635-1789*, vol. 1, A-H. Baltimore: The Johns Hopkins University Press.

Quarles, Benjamin. "Lord Dunmore as Liberator." *William and Mary Quarterly*, 3rd Series, 11 (1958): 495-505.

Reese, George, ed. *Proceedings in the Courts of Vice Admiralty of Virginia, 1698-1775*. Richmond: Virginia State Library, 1983.

Reps, John W. *Tidewater Towns*. Williamsburg: University of Virginia Press, 1972.

Robins, Sally Nelson. *History of Gloucester County, Virginia, and Its Families*. Richmond: West, Johnson & Co., 1893.

Ryan, Joanne Wood. "Gloucester County, Virginia, in the American Revolution." Unpublished M.A. thesis, College of William and Mary, 1978.

Sabine, Lorenzo. *Biographical Sketches of Loyalists of the American Revolution with an Historical Essay.* 1864. Reprint Port Washington, NY: Kennikat Press, 1966.

Sanchez-Saavedra, E.M. *A Guide to Virginia Military Organizations in the American Revolution, 1774-1787.* Richmond: Virginia State Library, 1978.

Scribner, Robert L. "Nemesis at Gwynn's Island." *Virginia Cavalcade* (Spring 1953): 43-49. Richmond: Virginia State Library.

Selby, John E. *Dunmore.* Ed. Edward M. Riley. Williamsburg: Virginia Independence Bicentennial Commission, 1977.

———. *The Revolution in Virginia 1775-1783.* Williamsburg: The Colonial Williamsburg Foundation, 1988.

Shuldham, Molyneux. *The Dispatches of Molyneux Shuldham, Vice-Admiral of the Blue and Commander-in-Chief of His Britannic Majesty's Ships in North America, January-July 1776.* Ed. Robert W. Neeser. New York: Naval Historical Society, 1913.

Smyth, Edward A. "Mob Violence in Prerevolutionary Norfolk, Virginia." Unpublished M.A. thesis, Old Dominion University, 1975.

Stewart, Robert Armistead, ed. "The Affair at Gwynn's Island." *The Researcher,* pub. ca. 1920.

Stewart, Robert Armistead. *History of Virginia's Navy of the Revolution.* Richmond: Dietz Press, 1933.

"Virginia Legislative Papers: The Case of John Wilkie of Gloucester." *Virginia Magazine of History and Biography* 15 (1908): 292-95.

Wright, Robert K., Jr. *The Continental Army.* Army Lineage Series. Washington, D.C.: Center of Military History, United States Army, 1983.

Wrike, Peter Jennings. "Mathews County Shipbuilding Patterns 1780-1860." Unpublished M.A. thesis, Old Dominion University, 1990.

Zimmer, Carmelin V., ed. "Selected Letters from the Parker Family Papers: The Correspondence of Margaret Parker." Unpublished M.A. thesis, Old Dominion University, 1977.

Index

Index